A Sting In The Tale

By

Anthony Milligan

To Kath,
with Luv & Hugz
xxx

Blocat Publications

Oldham

UK

ISBN 9781730794650

Contents

Beaches

We traipsed the five kilometres to Escargot D'or every sodding Sunday for lunch.

'Walking is good for your constitution my boy' mother declared with a wagging finger every time I even looked like complaining. Her real reason was that she didn't want father driving rat-arsed after he'd consumed too much local wine, which he invariably did.

I was allowed just one glass of watered-down wine. Oh, how I longed to have a couple of glasses of the rich red but no, they treated me like a damn kid; I'd be eighteen in two months for god's sake.

It was the same boring three weeks every year since I was five. Same tedious two-day drive down, same stopover, same 'idyllic' cottage and the same bloody empty beaches, Cote D'Snore I called the place. All the local youngsters had moved to the large towns for better-paid work. The only locals left all seemed to be older than god's granny.

On the day my life changed forever I decided to go for a long walk. A mile or so up the beach a headland jutted out into the sparkling Med, I'd never been there before. My parents were sprawled in deck chairs engrossed in their boring books as usual. 'I'm

1

going for a walk' I shouted from the gate.

'Bye darling don't be too long' mother called without looking up from her precious book.

'I'll be as long as I damn well please' I muttered.

Around the headland near a stand of stunted pine trees, nature called. I could have just stood on the empty beach and peed but, being an Englishman, I went behind a tree.

I had just finished when an angelic voice behind me said 'ello young man.' I was dumbstruck and stood frozen to the spot.

'Don't be embarrassed' came the lilting voice again 'everyone 'as to pee.'

I hurriedly tucked myself away without shaking, cursing inwardly as the last drops ran down my leg. I turned to behold the most beautiful creature I had ever seen. She was about my age, tall and slim with cornflower blue eyes, retroussé nose over full red lips and a mane of blonde thatch. She was stark naked.

I recoiled in astonishment, sitting down with a bump as my foot found a tree root. Her laughter tinkled like tiny silver bells. 'Oh, Englishman, you are so funny.'

I flushed, deeply embarrassed 'why are you sneaking up on people naked? I asked peevishly, my red face angled downwards. 'How did you know I was English, anyway?'

The tiny bells tinkled again 'by the way you are

dressed, of course, silly boy' she said 'those huge baggy shorts and the sandals with the stockings 'alf way up your skinny legs. As for that straw 'at I would not put it on the 'ead of the donkey.'

'My legs aren't skinny' I said sulkily 'they're slender.'

Her hand reached downward 'come, I 'elp you up' I extended my hand obediently. She pulled with remarkable strength and I found myself gawping open-mouthed at her amber beauty.

'What is the matter?' she asked 'ave you never seen a naked girl before?'

'Well, er, no' I blurted 'aren't you afraid you'll be arrested?'

'Silly Englishman, this is a naturist beach since last year. We are, ow you say, naturists.'

'Oh,' I said feeling stupid' 'Who are you with?'

'My family are camping behind those dunes' she pointed down the beach 'I 'ave come collecting firewood for the cooking. So, mon ami, what is your name?'

'I'm called Charlie.'

'Pleased to meet you Sharlee I'm Margot from Alsace, we are on a camping 'oliday, and you?'

I explained my plight as she listened sombrely 'Ah, parents can be most difficult; even mine' she smiled 'you would like to swim with me Sharlee, Oui?'

She had a totally unselfconscious grace, as

though she'd spent her entire life naked. I instantly fell in love with this feisty girl; my shyness melted. 'What about your firewood?'

'Later, it would be nice if you 'elped' she said, 'but first we swim, non?'

'Yes,' I said feeling relieved now because she would be covered by the water and I wouldn't have to control my wandering eyes. I stripped to my underpants.

She tut-tutted 'do all Englishmen wear those strange knickers?'

I blushed 'they're called underpants.'

'Well take them off' she ordered 'they look even more ridiculous than your shorts.'

'But....but' I stammered.

'Look' she stamped her tiny foot, pointing 'if I go around that 'eadland I put on the clothes, oui?' I nodded dumbly. 'So, if you come 'ere you take off the clothes, non?

I found being scolded by this bossy girl strangely exciting and we were alone so why not? I slipped off the offending underwear. My inhibitions instantly vanished as a sensation of pure joy washed over me. Never had I felt so liberated. We raced out to a distant rock, her lithe form cutting cleanly through the water.

Afterwards, we lay on the sand drying, asking each other about school, friends and our different lifestyles. Her father was a pharmacist with a shop near Strasbourg. Mine was a family solicitor. My mother was a housewife, hers taught English.

She suddenly gasped 'oh dear, the firewood, I forgot' we quickly went about gathering dead wood. 'Please, come and 'ave lunch with us' she pleaded 'my family will adore you.'

'Are you sure it'll be alright?'

'But of course, and my brother Sylvestre will be so envious' she giggled mischievously pointing downwards 'you are bigger than 'im.'

Her parents were delightful, her mother kissed my cheeks and, her father embraced me. Sylvestre shyly shook my hand. He was a good looking nineteen-year-old with the same brush of blonde hair as Margot. Lunch was superb with grilled sardines, cheese, olives and a huge salad. Wine and chatter flowed freely as I relaxed, wallowing in my new-found freedom.

Christophe, Margot's father, started talking about happenings in Europe. 'This German fellow 'itler' he said 'seems intent on starting another war. I don't know what will become of us if he does.' He looked towards Sylvestre his face bleak. Margot senior quickly changed the subject then Sylvestre produced a guitar and we sang.

The wine inevitably crept to my head. Fortunately, Margot's mum noticed and stopped my indulgence. 'Whatever would your parents think if we sent you 'ome drunk?' After that, she forced strong French coffee on me.

As the happiest afternoon of my life drew to a close, Margot held my hand and we walked back to where my clothes still lay. I found a piece of baling twine on the water line and bundled them up, reluctant to become their prisoner again. She kissed me on the lips 'You are such a sweet boy Sharlee and so 'andsome. Will you come again tomorrow?'

I returned her kiss clumsily my heart pounding 'Oh boy, yes' I said unable to believe my luck. As I departed my Joie de vie, her kiss and the wine conspired to lift me to towering heights of bliss. I was still deliriously happy and naked when I floated into the cottage. My parents stared aghast.

'What is the meaning of this *outrageous* exhibition?' my mother asked angrily. My father spluttered incoherently in the background his face crimson.

'I've become a naturist mother, that's all' I spread my arms wide and did a pirouette 'what's the matter? Have you never seen a naked boy before?' I went to my room leaving them shocked and speechless. I sank onto my bed giddy with happiness and masturbated joyously.

True to their middle-class Englishness my parents never mentioned the incident again although my father did make vague noises about being careful not to 'bring trouble home.'

Over the next two weeks, Margot and I met almost every day frolicking on the sand and in the sea like the overgrown children we were. My parents refused to visit the nudist camp, their inhibitions too deeply ingrained. We did all meet up once at Escargot D'dor for Sunday lunch though it wasn't a success. My folks were stiff and formal, their conversation stilted and faux polite.

My conversion to nudism was firmly established and things now started getting serious between Margot and me. I loved her with all the wild passion of youth.

One day whilst picnicking she stopped pretending not to notice my erection when we kissed. She took me in hand stroking and squeezing. I fondled her pert breasts and stroked her buttocks. She squirmed, moaning softly, guiding my hand to her secret folds. It didn't take long for either of us to climax, me crying out in ecstasy, she emitting little yelps of pleasure.

On the last full day of her holiday, Margot and I were leaving for our final picnic when her mother drew me aside. 'Margot has told me of her desire for you Charlie' she said 'please, be gentle with her' then she kissed my cheek tenderly, a tear in her eye. Naive young fool that I was I failed to grasp her meaning.

The picnic over, Margot cleared the food and plates from our blanket then held me close. She became very serious as she showed me the condoms, the first ones I'd ever seen. 'I want it to be you, Sharlee, 'oo makes me not the virgin' she whispered.

Making love with Margot was an experience that

stayed with me all my life. Yes, we were clumsy the first time but later we took it more slowly. We built up and up gently kneading, teasing until the final cascades of pleasure sent us into near delirium. I've been with women since who were very adept at pleasing me, but nothing compared with the soul-shattering ecstasy of my first time.

The next day Margot went home way up on the German border. We held each other close both shedding tears. 'Promise me you will write Sharlee; promise me you will come again next year. I love you so much.'

I promised and meant it with all my being; Margot had become my whole world.

I did return to France that next year, 1940, but to a very different beach, a grey beach. I was queuing waist deep in a grey sea waiting for a grey boat to rescue me from Dunkirk. Overhead grey Stuka dive bombers howled their banshee wail of death, stouping like grey metallic vultures dropping angry grey bombs on us. My whole world had turned grey.

Throughout the war whenever I felt afraid, which was often, I thought of Margot building fantasies around her. Her photo became dog-eared and worn but her memory always remained sharp, lifting my spirits.

It was five long years before I visited a French beach again this time in Normandy.

Epilogue:

I searched for Margot after the war, finding only an elderly great aunt in the small Alsace village of Uberach. What I discovered broke my heart. Her parents had been caught disseminating news from the BBC and were shot by the Gestapo. Margot escaped and became a resistance fighter building a fierce reputation. She had married a policeman and settled near Nice.

Sylvestre, poor boy, had been forced into German uniform and sent to the Russian front like so many young men of that region. He never came home.

I returned to England, became a solicitor and joined my father's practice. In 1949 I became chairman of the British Naturist Society. I never married although I had plenty of opportunities. None of the women I met could ever match up to the precious memories of my Margot.

In 1972, Margot, recently widowed, traced me. Although we were now fifty it was as though we were still teenagers, giggling and telling silly jokes. We were wed that same year.

Today, in our mid-nineties, we live in a modest cottage close to 'our' beach; we still occasionally walk hand in hand naked on the sands albeit a lot more slowly these days.

Ruby Tuesday

Looking from his office window Robert watched the old bag lady sit down on 'his' bench in the square below. She placed her baggage carefully about her then unwrapped a sandwich and began slowly to break it into pieces, a piece for herself and a piece for the birds.

A policeman approached her. Robert could see from his body language that he was not pleased to find her there. A sharp wave of his hand, a nod of her head, then she slowly picked up her bags. Her shoulders slumped in resignation as she trudged away. It seemed so cruel to Robert to shunt her away like that like she was so much detritus to be swept from the public gaze.

The following Tuesday, Robert was seated on the bench enjoying the spring sunshine. He was alone as usual, most of his colleagues thought him a little weird so chose not to eat with him. The old bag lady came and sat at the other end of his bench. 'Hello,' she said brightly.

'Hello yourself' he replied without enthusiasm.

'Eating on your own I see.'

'Yes, yes I prefer to' he said feeling defensive.

'I'm not into football or any sport for that matter you see so my work colleagues kind of hang together talking about these things.'

'What about the girls?' she asked.

'Oh, in our office there's only Stella who's under fifty and who is not either married or courting' he answered. Robert was feeling a little intruded upon and it irritated him.

'What about you?' he asked trying to steer the conversation away from himself. 'How come you live like this if that's not too rude a question?' If she could be nosy so could he.

'Circumstances' she sighed her voice sad, 'just circumstances.' Then she suddenly smiled at him displaying large gaps in her teeth.

'Ah yes,' Robert replied thinking of his own situation 'circumstances can get in the way.'

Robert still lived with his mother. His father had been dead these past four years. He'd love to have a place of his own but property prices being what they were in London it was virtually impossible to get a mortgage deposit together on his salary even if he could have afforded the repayments. Renting anywhere decent was out of his price range, too.

'I want to show you me jewels' she said, her voice radiating childish enthusiasm 'I'll show you because you're a nice boy, but I won't show anyone else.'

Oh God, he thought, she's a nutter. Why are the nutters always attracted to me?

'Sorry, I've got to be going now' he said briskly 'some other time perhaps, OK?' He half rose to leave when she spoke again.

'Oh, I understand' she said, her face falling 'I'm just a daft old woman soft in the head and here was me thinking you were different' there was an air of sad resignation in her voice that arrested him. He sat down again feeling embarrassed and ashamed.

'Er, well, OK, I don't have to go for a few minutes, I suppose.'

She broke into a broad smile, her dirty, deeply lined face glowing with pleasure. She delved into one of her numerous bags and came out with a battered coronation souvenir tin from which she prised the lid.

'There' she said handing them to him with an air of pride 'what do you think of those then?'

Robert looked into the tin and what he saw confirmed his worst fears the 'jewels' were mostly the sort of stuff to be found in Christmas crackers. 'Very nice' he said forcing a smile 'you had them long?'

'No' she replied 'only since I freed myself thirty odd years ago. How old are you?' she asked, suddenly changing the subject.

I'm thirty-six' he replied surprised yet again at the abrupt change of topic.

'You got anyone special? She queried looking straight into his eyes.

'No, there was a girl but… but, it didn't last' he let the words trail off he didn't want to think about Joan and that his inability to provide her with a house was the reason for their split, he still felt quite raw.

'What happened?' she asked sympathetically.

'I don't want to talk about it if you don't mind' he said brusquely 'and now I really must be off.

'With that, Robert rose, threw his sandwich paper into a nearby waste bin, and headed for his office.

'OK' she called after him 'I'll see you next Tuesday.'

The following week Robert saw the bag lady again he was sitting on the same bench thinking about his mother. He loved her dearly but wished she'd accept that he was grown man and could make his own decisions. He'd asked her repeatedly for just two sandwiches for lunch, but she always replied that he was a growing lad and should eat more.

'Hello there, are any of those sandwiches going spare?'

'Sure, help yourself' he said handing the old woman the packet, glad not to be throwing them to the pigeons. 'It's nice to see you again.'

'It's nice to see you too' she replied in her soft Irish brogue, 'one gets so little good conversation these days' she paused 'I used to enjoy conversations with all sorts highly intelligent people' she said in a sad voice.

'Why do you always come here on a Tuesday?' Robert asked, using her tactic of suddenly changing the direction of the conversation.

'Oh, I have a circuit' she replied 'Tuesday here, Wednesday the East End and so forth. People get used to seeing me around and I don't like to disappoint me public.'

Robert smiled, amused by the thought of an old bag lady having a public. She was a lovely, harmless old soul he thought, and her blarney was always welcome. She was like a breath of fresh air, cheering him up and lightening the monotony of his day. He quite looked forward to Tuesdays now, they were different if only for half an hour or so. He was bemused and beguiled by her in equal measure with her sudden and often wild changes of direction in her conversation. He wondered to himself what her background really was and how come she'd ended up living like this.

'And you had great conversations in your former life?'

'Yes, oh yes' she said her pale eyes shining 'we always had interesting visitors up at the big house. Father was a scientist you know, he had all sorts of clever friends.'

Robert was intrigued she did have a rather refined Irish accent and mostly spoke as though she was still in contact with reality. But then he remembered her jewels and sighed.

'I call myself Ruby now but back then I was Lady Rowena Mary O'Malley-Fitzpatrick of Connedown.' A small tear appeared at the corner of her eye and Robert could feel nothing but pity for this poor woman. OK, so she was as mad as a barking duck, but she believed her story, it was as real to her as her distress was to him.

He looked at her wrinkled old face and washed out blue eyes feeling deep compassion for this hapless victim of life. Whatever she was or had been she was still a human being and a very vulnerable one at that.

He found his voice at last 'What happened to make you so unhappy, Ruby?'

She smiled brightly 'Oh, I'm happy enough with my lot now' she said 'I had a gloriously happy childhood but then, when I was eighteen, I fell in love with the wrong person. We were found out you see' she sniffed as if about to burst into tears and he reached out and took her grubby hand. 'We were caught 'flagrante delicto' as they say, in the silver cupboard so we were, both naked to the waist, kissing passionately and fondling each other's breasts.'

Robert felt a slight shock at this revelation but held his peace it was nineteen sixty-four for god's sake this sort of thing was becoming more accepted nowadays by the young at least.

'Father hit the roof.'

She told how he had declared that these were the passions of the devil, they were abhorrent in the sight of God and deviant in the extreme. 'The other girl, Debra, was our new parlour maid you see. She'd only been with us a month or so but as soon as we saw each other we knew' she paused in sad reflection for a moment 'Debra's father was summoned, and he took her home in disgrace that very afternoon.'

'What happened to her? Have you met her since?

'No, she was taken to see the priest who prayed for her and said a mass for her salvation then a suitable young man was found, and she was forced to marry. She hanged herself a year later. I was sent to a convent home to be cured. Not the normal Irish home for wayward girls, of course, I was from a good family you see.

Robert was incredulous 'cured?' he exclaimed 'how the hell were they supposed to do that?'

'By constant prayer and deep contemplation upon the crucified Christ who died for all our sins,' Ruby said it mechanically as if repeating what someone had drummed into her.

'Good Lord.'

'The only other girl there was called Sheila' Ruby looked wistful, her mouth drooping 'she was the same age as me and eight months pregnant. The father had run off to America, she was just another poor fool who fell in love' she sighed and paused, her eyes held a watery, distant look 'I remember when she had the baby it was in the early hours of the morning and by breakfast time the baby was gone, sent for adoption.

I can still hear her screaming for her child. Ireland was a very conservative place in those days; it still is for that matter.'

'It sounds more like a sanctuary of the devil' Robert said aghast.

'The Devil? We had a strict routine that saved us from him' Ruby said 'we rose at five a.m. and prayed for half an hour then went back to bed until seven thirty. Ablutions followed and then a priest came to say morning mass and give communion before a breakfast of porridge. Always porridge it was except on Sundays when we had a boiled egg with it. We worked in the vegetable garden or sewed until we said the angelus at twelve. Lunch was soup and dry bread with a cup of tea. More work until five when we prayed again and sang hymns for an hour. After that, we read the bible and said the Rosary until supper at seven. We went to bed at eight and we read and prayed for our sins to be forgiven. Lights went out at nine.

'Good God' Robert gasped 'how long did that go on for?'

'It was supposed to be for six months, but mother died suddenly after I'd been there for three months' she sounded bitter and tears started flowing, filling the crags of her face like tiny silver rivers as she went on: 'Father sent a letter telling me it was my fault and that she had died of shame and a broken heart caused by my wickedness. I was not allowed to return home again nor was I welcome at her funeral. I was never to contact my brother, sister or any family member again, ever.' Her hands clasped and unclasped in her lap, the pain in her eyes all too apparent.

Robert's heart lurched, and he felt like crying at the sheer cruelty of it all. The poor woman was wrenched from her family and friends and cast aside as worthless simply because she was homosexual.

Good god, did her people believe that being homosexual was a choice that one made?

Robert simply didn't know what to make of her story one moment Ruby was an intelligent woman making perfect sense and the next she was lost to wild fluctuations in both thought process and speech. One thing was for sure, though, it was real enough to her.

'Has there been no one else in your life since Ruby?'

Oh yes, she said, cheering up. When twenty-one I declared myself cured and left the Sisters of Perpetual Punishment, as I called them. I had a little money and some of my mother's jewellery, so I took the boat to Liverpool. I got work as a lady's companion for a while, but it was tedious, and that old style was fast dying out. Then I met Amber and we fell in love. We moved to London for work and what they called the Bohemian lifestyle, but the war broke out and we had to take jobs in different places. I guess we just drifted apart.'

Her face changed, and she smiled broadly 'did you ever watch the changing of the guard at Buckingham Palace?' she suddenly asked. 'I go there most Fridays in the winter' she said, skewing wildly from the topic of conversation again 'there's just too many tourists in the summer.' Just as quickly she reverted to the original topic.

'After the war, I met Julia and we moved to the North, but we were hounded out of one place after another when they found out we were a couple. Eventually, I couldn't find work and started drinking. One thing led to another and here I am.'

'Do you still drink Ruby?'

'No, I gave it up when I found a place at the hostel. They were very kind and really helped me with my problems but then the place closed through lack of funds and we had to move out.'

Robert looked at his watch and was shocked 'Good lord Ruby, I should be at work. See you next Tuesday OK?' and with that, he hurried away. That night he couldn't sleep for thinking about Ruby and what, if anything, he could do to help her.

The following Tuesday was a cold and wet. They sat in a bus shelter out of the wind sharing his sandwiches. She as talking lucidly about Harold Wilson and the recent change of government when she suddenly clutched her chest, groaned and fell against him. An ambulance was called, and Robert accompanied her to the hospital.

When Robert visited Ruby that evening, she was conscious but looked very weak. 'I want you to have me jewels Robert' she told him. 'promise me you'll look after them when I'm gone.'

'Just rest now dear Ruby' he said gently. 'I'll take care of everything until you're better' he held her hand, he could see she was sinking fast. Her eyes closed, and she breathed softly for half an hour. Then her breathing became ragged and she opened her eyes one last time.

'Goodbye Robert' she whispered, 'thank you for being my friend' she let out a final sighing breath and was gone.

Later, a staff nurse handed him her 'jewel' box. 'She said you'd want these, and there's a photograph too.' she handed him a tattered old black and white postcard size photo. Looking at the picture Robert was astounded, it was unmistakably that of a very young Ruby dressed, it appeared, for a ball. She wore a flowing, elegant ball gown and long-sleeved gloves. There was a tiara in her hair and at her throat was what looked like a large diamond pendant on a choker. She held a small evening bag and from her wrist dangled a dance card. she looked stunning.

Back in his room that night Robert wept bitterly for Ruby and her life destroyed by blind prejudice. How could the people who were supposed to love her have treated her like that?

At Ruby's funeral, he was the only mourner. On returning home Robert, who had put the jewel box aside, now opened it and smiled at the junk inside. He stirred it with his forefinger until one item caught his eye. It looked vaguely familiar but was caked in filth and looked badly tarnished.

Suddenly he picked up the trinket and the photo and compared the two. There was no doubt at all it was the same pendant that had been around her throat all those years before. He hurried to the bathroom, took a nail brush and began carefully removing the dirt of decades. The whole thing took on a brilliance that told him that these were real diamonds.

When the man in Hatton Gardens told him what it was worth Robert nearly fainted.

'Are you sure?' he asked hardly able to believe his ears.

'Oh quite' the jeweller had said 'It's Russian made, seven and a half carats of the best stones I've ever seen, mounted in platinum and bearing the Faberge mark; an absolutely stunning piece.'

Robert Winston Brewer passed away in two thousand and thirteen at the age of eighty-five. His daughter knew that she had been named Rowena

Mary after an Irish noblewoman her father told her had once known. It was not until she read his diaries that she learned the full story. She'd always believed the house she had grown up in so loved and cherished had been named Ruby Tuesday after a favourite pop song her father had always sung.

Attention to Detail

Ahmed watched fascinated as the bomb maker worked slowly and methodically across the table from him.

Ali Wazir finished shaping the charge of plastic explosives and looked up, giving a humourless smile as he peeled off his surgical gloves. His dark eyes flashed with satisfaction 'when the bomb is complete there will also be five kilos of ball bearing to increase the effect he said, 'the carnage will be great.'

Muszra Azziz was the third man present, he was the group's leader. A small, dark-eyed man with a thick moustache and a smallpox pitted face. He lit a Turkish cigarette.

'Pay attention, Ahmed, this is the mobile phone that will cause the detonation. First, you must take it to work and test for a strong signal' he handed Ahmed the simple pay-as-you-go instrument.

'I'm sure it will be fine, Muszra.'

'Check it anyway, Ahmed. When you plant the device first switch on the phone, only when it is up and running will you connect it and throw this arming switch, OK?' Azziz pointed to an electronic box with a red LED and a single switch. 'Once this switch is activated it cannot be switched off without detonating the explosives.'

'I understand Muszra, though I would be willing to detonate it personally and enter paradise.'

'Your zeal is noted Ahmed, but we have other work for you. Engineers with your skills can gain entry to many places and we have other targets. Be patient.'

Ahmed examined his toolbox 'it fits so well Muszra, very precise and I still have room for my tool tray on top.'

John Patchett, chief maintenance engineer at Aircol Max Plc regarded his protégé with admiration. Ahmed was quick to learn, an instinctive engineer. His beloved machines would be in good hands when he retired. The gentle older man had learned to accept Ahmed's peculiarities like his insistence on taking his tools home every night, of sitting on the toolbox to eat at lunch and at break time, snubbing the works canteen.

'In my country' Ahmed had explained 'if a man lost his tools, he would have no means to support his family. It would be a terrible disaster.'

'I wish you were as conscientious at keeping up the service and repair logs Uthman, you have a whole batch to bring up to date.' John sighed, he couldn't understand why Ahmed let the paperwork slip. Unless John kept on to him about it, it would never be completed. It was just another of Ahmed's idiosyncrasies he had learned to live with.

John also puzzled Ahmed by doing him little kindnesses at every opportunity. He had brought him a cushion from home to put atop his toolbox to sit on. Why? He also covered for him whilst he went to pray and never complained even when it inconvenienced him. The old man never shirked getting down on his knees to work in awkward corners of some of the machines. He could have made him do it and save his ageing body. The man was a fool and would die with the rest of the fools.

Ahmed drove a dilapidated old car even though he could afford a much better one. 'Western materialism doesn't interest me' he told John when he remarked on it one day, 'it's a good car, only the locks do not work everything else is fine. Who would steal such a car anyway?'

John had not mentioned the car again considering it just another of Ahmed's peculiar attitudes.

'Right, Ahmed, we've been given the task of building a platform for the opening of the new wing and installing the speaker system, apparently, the Minister is to make a speech.'

Aircol Max Plc had recently made a breakthrough in the fuel systems of jet engines making them run cleaner by almost 10% and for minimal cost, too. Such was the potential that the new extension had been built to accommodate this development. It was to be opened by the government's environmental minister herself. This was a chance Ahmed and his group could not ignore. The opportunity to assassinate a government minister and several dignitaries as well as up to two hundred highly skilled engineers could not be passed up.

The company supplied the civil aviation industry. It had no political or military affiliations. This would be just another routine job for the Minister Ms Sally Goldsworthy. She did around twenty of this type of ceremony every year. Nothing about it was controversial; there was no particular security threat and no grounds for anyone in high places to worry. It was just uncomplicated every day ministerial work.

Ms Goldsworthy had insisted on the minimum of fuss for her visit. She would arrive at eleven forty-five, meet the directors and senior staff then proceed to the new department. There she would make a short speech then uncover the wall plaque declaring the new wing open. After a light lunch in the boardroom, she would depart no later than twelve thirty. Her aides had called weeks before to discuss such things as security, lunch menus, toilet facilities and other nitty-gritty details that accompanied ministerial visits. Everything had been thrashed out to the satisfaction of her team.

'We will have to build the platform at least two

feet high John I've checked, and the minister is only five feet one inch tall.'

John was impressed 'that's great research Ahmed, well done. By the way, have you completed those maintenance logs yet?'

'Soon, John, I promise.'

'It will need to be soon Ahmed; the general manager was asking about them earlier. I can't keep putting him off. You really need to pay more attention to these details.'

Their work on the platform progressed well, two small steps and a handrail were built, and Ahmed brought some blue velvet cloth to skirt the front and sides of platform's base. It looked like a very professional job. A speaker system was brought in to ensure the assembled workforce heard the minister's speech.

Ahmed watched as Wazir completed the bomb. It consisted of five kilos of Semtex1A, the most powerful of commercial explosives. Wazir had lined the bottom half of Ahmed's toolbox with half-inch ball bearings superglued to the sides. The explosive was then added turning the toolbox into lethal Claymore mine. In the confines of the foyer of the new extension, the effect would be devastating.

Ahmed knew no one would suspect the maintenance engineers going about their business. He would leave the toolbox under the platform at the last minute.

The minister would be standing right above it to make her speech. He himself would leave on the pretext of having a dental appointment. He'd even made an actual appointment with his dentist just in case anyone checked up on him. As Azziz had said, attention to detail was the key to success.

Wazir finally finished, replacing the tray of tools on top. Once more it looked like an engineer's toolbox.

Ahmed knew John was very conscientious and would stay with him throughout the installation of the PA system. He had sabotaged a machine in the main workshop by over tightening a bearing. He knew it was a machine John loved to work on. Ahmed should be left alone in the new foyer for at least a few minutes and that was all he needed. If not, he had another plan.

On the day of the grand opening, John and Ahmed set up the microphone and rigged it to the speakers, tested it and did one or two other jobs. The Minister's security woman came around and checked the room. She looked under the platform using a torch. She then went through the doors of the new wing, doing more checks. Satisfied, she left leaving the two engineers tidying up wires.

'What's the matter, Ahmed?' You look as nervous as a cat in the vets.'

'Oh, it's my dental appointment this afternoon, John' he answered, 'I really hate going to the dentist, it terrifies me.'

John nodded his understanding, he also hated going to the dentists.

As the time for the visit got nearer, they gave the microphone system one last test. Ahmed's nervousness seemed to be increasing by the minute, surely that bearing must have burnt out by now? He had foreseen the possibility of having to kill John, there could be no blood spilt to cause questions. Both John's corpse and the bomb would fit under the platform, so disposal of John's body was not a problem. He reached into his pocket for the sash cord garrotte he'd brought as a contingency plan and moved behind the older man.

John's phone rang. 'Yes? Oh, I see, I'll be right along, he turned to Ahmed 'I have to go, mate, the big milling machine's playing up again.'

Ahmed breathed a sigh of relief as his hand released the garotte. Once alone he quickly armed the device then pushed his toolbox under the platform. It was time to be off.

Walking through the factory Ahmed bumped into the Mark Dutton the general manager, he was not a happy man. He was carrying a bunch of maintenance logs Ahmed recognised as his.

'I'll need these signing before you go anywhere Ahmed, my office now please.'

'I'm sorry Mark, but I have a dental appointment, they'll be upset if I'm late.'

Dutton was having none of it 'not as upset as I'll be. It'll take just a few minutes Ahmed and I must insist that in future you pay more attention to these things.' Ahmed reluctantly complied as he still had a few minutes in hand and he couldn't afford to raise suspicion.

Hurrying to his car Ahmed drove to the rendezvous on a hill half a mile away that overlooked the factory. The lane was deserted because it led nowhere, the farmhouse it once served had long been demolished. It was one of those desolate places used by fly-tippers and prostitutes who brought clients there after dark.

Ahmed was first there despite his delay. He checked his watch and saw that he was still a minute early. The others arrived on time and drove up behind him.

Getting out of his car Ahmed went and sat in the back of the BMW driven by Abdul Azziz. 'All set?' Azziz asked.

'Yes,' Ahmed replied, 'I paid full attention to every detail.'

Azziz lit a cigarette and sat silently turning a set of worry beads in his left hand he closed his eyes and drew smoke deeply into his lungs then he slowly exhaled. Beside him sat Wazir who was staring straight ahead, rocking backwards and forwards mumbling prayers.

Cigarette finished, Azziz watched through

powerful binoculars 'OK' he hissed, 'the official cars are arriving.'

He handed Ahmed a phone 'to you, Ahmed, must go the ultimate honour of detonating the device' he said solemnly 'this is your first operation and you have done well my friend.'

He took the Minister's schedule from his pocket and read it for the tenth time 'eight minutes to enter, meet and greet' he said, his voice cold and steady 'then one minute to walk to the new building followed by a seven-minute speech to the workers so that's twelve minutes to detonation, right in the middle of her speech' he smirked and lit another cigarette. He was enjoying himself. In the back of the car, Ahmed was deep in thought. It was right, he believed, that the infidel should be taught a lesson in blood, but he hoped John would stay with his machine and not attend the opening. Despite his beliefs, Ahmed found to his surprise that he didn't want the old man to die.

'One minute' the voice of Azziz cut through his thoughts. 'bring up contacts' Azziz ordered 'select Wazir and await my command.'

Ahmed held the phone in trembling hands. 'Wait….wait....' said Azziz looking at his watch. Time seemed to stand still for Ahmed. In the front passenger seat, Wazir continued rocking back and forth, praying louder now, a fixed stare in his eyes.

'Now' barked Azziz and Ahmed brought his

thumb down on the dialling button. He heard the phone beep beeping out the number, a slight pause then the phone made its connection. The bomb detonated with its full lethal force.

John rang Ahmed's number; the phone went straight to voicemail. Thinking he must still be at the dentist's he left a message. 'Hi Ahmed, listen, mate, I left my glasses on the platform and when I went back for them, I noticed some tape you used had come unstuck on those microphone wires that crossed the floor. When I bent down to replace it I noticed you'd left your toolbox under the platform. I was told you were in with Dutton, so I took it to the car park and popped it in your car boot old son. John's voice took on a humorous note 'That dentist must really have got to you rattled old son, I've never known overlook a small detail like your toolbox before.'

The Village Ram

Her slender body clad only in a tiny bikini bottom left little to his fevered imagination. What was she? Nineteen, twenty perhaps? Her cute retrousse nose was set above the baby pink pillows of her lips, she was face framed by her wild blonde thatch. Best of all he liked her pert breasts, so firm, entirely self-supporting, the nipples were taught and deep pink.

Her bikini bottoms stretched taut across her boyish hips, touching lightly on her stomach just above her mons pubis leaving a shady gap at either side that seemed to invite his probing fingers to explore further.

God, she's beautiful he thought feeling a strong stirring in his loins.

He stared too long and she, sensing his attention, pulled down her sunglasses and peered over her book her cornflower blue eyes looking inquisitively into his. He hurriedly averted his gaze and she smiled impishly. She was still smiling when he glanced back. Surprised, he managed a furtive little grin as she replaced her shades returning to her book. It was the briefest of incidents, but it fired him to seek more, a chat, a drink and then his particular brand of seduction. She was now marked for conquest.

He didn't seem to mind The girls at his local massage parlour had nicknamed him 'The Village Ram' because his lovemaking was brutal and crude. He liked what he called his 'specials' which usually entailed the girls being hurt and humiliated what they charged as long as they satisfied his lust. He called it 'cooking his cock' and laughed if he reduced one of the girls to tears. He was a bastard, yes, but he was a rich bastard who paid well so they indulged him.

Robert Bight was forty-two and had started to grow jowly and thicker around his midriff, a result of his self-indulgent lifestyle. He still believed himself handsome, God's gift to women. He looked at her again she looked so sweet, this girl deep in her book tongue tip on lip, so young so naïve. He imagined what it would be like when he drove his cock deep into her young body. She'd smiled at him, hadn't she? So she must fancy him. Anyway, he reasoned, lots of young girls fancied older men. The smile had convinced him. Yes, she's up for it he told himself. If not he'd get her too drunk to stop him. One way or another she'd be his cock candy.

She rose, stretched her lovely long limbs and dived into the pool. He watched as she swam swiftly, lithely to the far end then turned effortlessly swimming back the twenty-five metres under the surface. He started to plan. First, see what book she was reading always a good way to start a conversation. He sidled past her sun lounger "Fifty Shades of Grey" now that was interesting. Buying a beer from the poolside bar he wandered back to his lounger thinking stratagem.

It was six months now since Tania had thrown him out and Robert had had to make even greater use of massage parlours, sleazy dating sites, online porn and 'madam palm.' Tania had finally tired of his constant, overbearing demands for sex and his rough 'rapists' approach when she demurred. She knew about the prostitutes, too. Now, he believed, she wanted half of his assets. She was still a company director of course because she was brilliant with finance, but he'd done the donkey work getting the company off the ground. He knew underworld people at the gym. When he got back off holiday, he would make enquiries about disappearing her or maybe an apparent suicide? He snapped his mind back to the present bugger her he thought his holiday agenda required his total attention.

Robert saw the girl again at dinner chatting animatedly to two other girls at a nearby table. He watched surreptitiously as her pretty mouth smiled, pouted and laughed exposing even white teeth as the conversation flowed. God, how he'd enjoy screwing her.

Later, entering the bar, he saw her sitting alone

on a barstool. Seizing his opportunity, he sauntered across 'large scotch and ice please.' He glanced to his left pretending he'd just recognised her. 'Oh hello,' he quipped 'so this is where you hang out when you're not modelling eh?'

She laughed at the cheesy compliment blushing slightly curtaining her eyes with her long lashes 'I'm not a model silly' she said looking flattered nonetheless 'I'm a student.'

He moved closer but avoided invading her personal space, easy does it he thought. 'Not out with your friends tonight? '

'No I have a bit of a headache so I decided on a couple of drinks and an early night.'

An early night fucking you would suit me just fine darling he thought smiling to hide his lust.

They sipped their drinks chatting about Uni and how lovely the resort was. Her name was Chloe and no, she didn't have a boyfriend at the moment. She thought younger men were crass bores, so obvious in their desires and sulky when rejected. Robert's loins stirred at the news.

Eventually, she said 'if you'll excuse me, Robert, I need a little air' she arose without waiting for an answer and wandered through the patio doors to the deserted pool.

He slowly finished his drink then followed her. She was hard to spot sitting on a sun lounger at the far end of the pool in almost complete darkness. He circumnavigated the pool stealthily keeping to the shadows. 'I thought you were going to bed' he said feigning surprise.

Startled she gasped 'Oh, oh it's you Robert I was just admiring the new moon, so romantic don't you think?

He sat down beside her 'accidentally' brushing her shoulder. She winced 'Ouch! Sorry, Robert, I got too much sun today and I can't reach with the after-sun cream.'

'Would you like me to...er?' his voice trailed off feigning embarrassment.

'Oh that would be great thank you' she enthused her innocent smile sending shivers through him. From her handbag, she produced a small bottle of cream then bent forward pulling up her top from behind. She wasn't wearing a bra and the sight of her under breast made him start to harden. Oh yes! Another lamb to the slaughter he thought.

Practised fingertips gently eased cream into her back for some time then he moved slowly up to her neck and shoulders kneading expertly. She moaned softly 'Oh that's so nice Robert.'

He reached for her breast but she brushed his hand aside 'Please Robert' she protested pulling her top down 'you're a fast worker and no mistake but she was still smiling. She drew her bag onto her knees in a defensive gesture then. fumbling in it she took out some sweets popping one into her mouth.

She smiled 'Bon-Bons, want one?' she proffered the bag then pouted when he refused. 'They're specially imported from India they kill horrid whiskey breath' she said sulkily then, more brightly, she added 'they're also a mild stimulant' she winked mischievously holding out the bag again. He took one sucking on it with a lewd smile. Things were going well.

The usual routine with this little strumpet he thought then dump her and play the field again. In his mind, he ran through his master plan. He'd done this before lots of times on holiday and it had always worked. A soft seduction and a gentle fuck tonight then back to his room. In the early hours, he'd give her a real rough screwing squeezing her breasts hard. If she complained he'd humbly apologize reducing himself to tears if need be and spin her a tale of woe about what a hard time he was having with his ex-wife

They always forgave him and this one would be no different. Later, still playing the sincere penitent, the gentle seduction once again this time he'd take her from the rear over a pile of pillows. At the last second, he'd retrieve his hidden lube, slip off the condom, lubricate his cock and ram it hard up her arse. God, he loved doing that. The shock, the surprise, the pain until his shaft breached the sphincter and pushed all the way up. They were usually calmer then it didn't hurt as much, becoming easier to handle.

The last one he'd done (Was it Joanne?) screamed so loud he'd had to put her in a Half Nelson pushing her face into the mattress as she fought like a tigress. He had wrapped a brawny arm around her slender hips pinning her like a moth on a board whilst he screwed her hard and fast until he finally came then she'd fainted.

Later, the tears of shame streaming down her face, she had staggered from his room. She'd cut short her holiday and flown home the same day. They never told anyone these young inexperienced girls being far too ashamed to reveal that they'd got drunk and slept with a debauched old lecher. God how he loved the feeling of power, of control.

She was talking now, smiling happily. He slipped his arm around her and gently nibbled her ear. Chloe moaned softly and leaned into him. He found her breasts and stroked lightly, expertly causing slivers of delight to run through her. He was pleasantly surprised to find she was going commando. His fingers found her clitoris. Christ, he thought it must be an inch long and as hard as my cock. He wet his fingers in her and ever so softly brushed the tip of her protuberance. She gave little 'Ah's' of pleasure as she gyrated to his fondling fingers. Hell, he thought, these young girls were so damned easy and this one is great.

'Robert' she whispered, 'I want to show you

something very special' and pushed him gently back on the lounger. His eyebrows rose in query 'it's something very special indeed' she said teasingly.

She was over him now bare-breasted, nuzzling his neck lightly stroking his chest with her hard nipples. He responded stroking buttocks in light, slow circles. She unzipped his trousers fondling his hardness. Then the rest of their clothing fell away. She magically conjured up a condom and slid it expertly over his manhood. 'Now baby' she cooed 'this will be the best experience of your life I guarantee it.'

He relaxed, let her have her way. There's a first time for everything he thought and who knows, it could be great. She took him into her mouth slowly until every inch had been accommodated. She produced the powerful meditative "aum" vibration deep in her throat as she ran her full lips up and down his rock-hard shaft. The vibrations built until every fibre of his being was pulsating with pleasure sending him crazy with ecstasy. Then, as he approached his peak, she sat up. He groaned wanting her to finish him.

She smiled straddling him 'Not yet baby' she whispered, 'Chloe hasn't finished with naughty Robert just yet.' then she was riding him, slowly at first, then gradually speeding up using her pelvic floor muscles expertly to tease and squeeze. She knew to the second when to ease off to stop him coming then leaving him pleading 'Chloe, for God's sake, *please*.'

She worked him to a peak again and again. At last, he could stand it no more 'please,' he pleaded 'Jesus, finish me off.' She said nothing just gave him a dazzling smile, tightening her muscles hard she rode him fiercely. His breathing shortened, rasping and gasping as he gulped air. They climaxed together him crying 'Yes, yes, oh Jesus yes! she making little whimpering noises deep in her throat having spasm after rolling spasm. She subsided then lying on top of him for several long minutes pinning passionately allowing his now flaccid cock to slide out of her. He looked up at her glassy eyed, his breathing still coming in short gasps. She picked up his arm and let go, pleased to see that it flopped to his side 'I'll tell you a story Robert' she said seriously 'When I was fourteen my father died and mum took me on a spiritual retreat to India. One night, walking back to our ashram from the village, a group of men attacked us. Mother and I were gang raped vaginally, orally and anally.' She paused looking sad 'mother ended her days in a mental hospital and I needed three years of therapy to recover. The men were from wealthy families, bribes were paid, and no one was prosecuted' she continued 'the Guru at our ashram was outraged; he was an expert practitioner of Ayurvedic medicine. He gave me a secret formula for a rare poison which kills efficiently producing all the symptoms of a heart attack and is virtually untraceable. In tiny doses, like the one in your Bon-Bon, it causes slow paralysis which wears off after an hour or two. Until it does you can feel, hear and see but cannot move or speak.'

She strokes his head like he was a fractious child that needed comforting. 'That's why I screwed you Robert, to give the stuff time to work.' She fumbled in her bag, producing a large dildo. 'Guess what comes next Robert?' She smiled mischievously 'some of the anal pleasure you so love to bestow on others.' Strapping it on she looked around to make sure there were no witnesses then rolled him onto his stomach. He made a few small gurgling noises as she penetrated him and rode him mercilessly, his eyes streaming tears of pain, but he was helpless to stop her.

When she had finished, Cloe tipped the sun lounger rolling him off. She dragged him to the poolside then continued 'you see Robert you went skinny dipping, slipped on the water from the shower here and banged your head on the poolside falling into the water unconscious. The post mortem will confirm drowning as the cause of death, the toxicology report will show you've a few drinks. The poison requires very sophisticated tests so will not show up. With such an obvious cause of death, no one will be looking for it anyway.

Lifting his head, Cloe smashed it down hard onto

the tiled edge of the pool smiling mirthlessly as his gaping mouth screamed soundlessly. 'Don't worry Robert you won't suffer long I'm good at this having practised on four Indian gentlemen.'

She watched the terror in his bulging eyes with deep satisfaction then kissed him and said sweetly 'goodbye Robert' before holding him under the water watching his mouth make weak pleading shapes as his last breath gushed from his lungs.

Afterwards Chloe took a shower enjoying the hot cleansing deluge on her skin. It was over. They may ask her questions tomorrow, but her story was ready. She would say that in the bar he'd invited her to go swimming. She had refused because he looked and sounded creepy and way too old for her anyway.

Lying naked on her bed she took the throw-away phone and made a call.

'Hello Chloe'

'Hi Tania it's done. The company's all yours. You can deposit the balance of my fee now.'

A Cantankerous Owd Git

The old man shuffled into the dark side street. He didn't like it but it was the only way to his flat. He saw a dark shadow detach itself from the deeper gloom of a derelict shop doorway. The shadow turned into a swaggering youth. His way barred the old man stopped. The youth held out his hand 'give.'

'Got nowt lad. '

The young man stepped in to within two feet. The old man sensed rather than saw the lightening movement and heard the vicious click of a flick knife.

Albert Jackson eyed the youth calmly. At seventy eight, he had recently lost his beloved wife of fifty two years. He didn't much care if he lived or died but this little shit was not having his money easily. Could he remember the old stuff? Could he still use it?

The mugger was too far away, his reflexes were nowhere near as fast as his opponent's and Jackson knew it. He had his two hundred pounds winter fuel allowance on him and he was loath to give up. Bollocks, he thought, I'll give it a go.

'If you don't put that knife away son I'll take it

off you and shove it up your arse.'

The man's eyes flash in astonishment. If he struck now Jackson was dead.

'What the fuck?'

Jackson raised his right hand in a defensive gesture. His fingertips brushing his top lip; his hand was now where it needed to be.

The snarling youth grabbed Jackson by the lapel, jerking him hard, the knife raised above his head. Jackson could see his eyes now full of hate, his breath stank of stale tobacco. The next few seconds would tell.

His hand was at the right height, the strike distance now a mere foot. His fist flew into the man's throat as Jackson stepped sharply forward to follow through. The man gagged, spinning away as the Communist Terrorist had done decades before in Malaya. The mugger went down on hands and knees clutching at his throat, legs splayed.

Jackson took his time, anchored his left leg, and aimed his kick through the man's legs. He felt the meaty thud as shin met testicles. He heard with satisfaction the man's choking noises go up an octave as he slumped into the foetal position.

The knife was lying at his feet. He took out his handkerchief 'a promise is a promise lad.'

Grasping the mugger's knife in his handkerchief Jackson slashed the man's trousers from belt to gusset. Inserting the blade Jackson thrust hard and kept pushing until only the last half inch of the handle was left protruding from the bleeding anus. The mugger jerked spasmodically his choked off screams growing fainter as his feet scrabbled feebly on the pavement.

'If you're going to target pensioners lad, best you stick to women.' He made his unhurried way home, checked his clothes for blood then burned his handkerchief. After downing a large scotch Jackson went to bed.

The knock came just after lunch next day 'Mr Jackson? Detective Constable Wilfred Redding sir' he flashed his warrant card 'I have a few questions for you about an incident in Peckmore Street last evening.'

'Really?' Jackson's face was a picture of innocent puzzlement. 'You'd best come in then.'

Redding refused the offer of tea and sat precariously on a rickety upright chair.

'Mr Jackson, a man was killed near here last night . You were seen on the CCTV entering Peckmore street at ten oh two sir.'

'Oh, so they've finally got around to fixing it eh? Not before bloody time either.'

'CCTV's been working again for the last month I'm told sir.'

'How come you've got no one for mugging old Mrs McClaren two weeks ago then?'

'We're still working on that case sir.'

'Don't you have CCTV images of that incident then?'

'Camera was on the blink that night sir and it only covers the junction not the whole street. We'll catch him, though, never fear. Now….'

'Oh I don't fear officer, I'm too bloody old for fear.'

'Anyway, sir, did you see anything unusual or suspicious?

'No.'

'No ? You didn't see anyone else there?'

'Yes, there was a man curled up on the ground. I thought he was either a junkie or a drunk.'

'And you didn't think to report it sir?'

'How long have you been policing round here son?'

'I'm new here, just a week.'

'Ah, that explains your ignorance then' Jackson rasped. He saw the officer flinch at his barb. He looked him square in the eye. 'It pays to mind your own damned business in this neighbourhood.'

'So, you saw nothing else, then?'

'It's always dark on Peckmore Street mate, council seem to have run out of light bulbs. They blame the cutbacks.' He deliberately put passion into his voice 'the streets where the councillors live are always well lit, though. Bastards.'

Redding sensed a rant coming on. The neighbours had said he was an old soldier and a cantankerous old sod. 'Yes sir, but that's not a matter for now.'

The interview concluded shortly afterwards.

A week later all the CCTV surrounding Peckmore Street had been painstakingly analysed.

'I tell you Sarge, apart from the victim, Jackson was the only one in that area for at least half an hour before Waldo Snaith's time of death.' Redding looked perplexed 'also, timing Jackson's progress from other cameras he passed, if he'd have kept up the same pace he should have left Peckmore street one full minute earlier than he did.'

Detective Sergeant Lucking looked sceptical 'Mr Jackson is seventy eight for god's sake with no previous. I can't see it Wilf.'

'I know Sarge, but he was the only one there. I've also checked his military record. He was in quite a lot of trouble in his early career, fighting mostly. He was, however, awarded the Military Medal for action in Malaya against Communist Terrorists.'

'That was a helluva long time ago Wilf, he has to be well past it now.'

'He was twenty at the time Sarge and no stranger to killing. I've got his citation here.' He handed the print-out to Lucking.

On June the 2nd 1958 Private Albert Jackson of 'A' Company,2nd Battalion the Coldstream Guards was part of a patrol hunting Communist Terrorists

in an area north of Tampin, Negri Sembilan, Malaya. At the end of the patrol his unit had almost reached their base when, rounding a bend in the Jungle, they were confronted by a superior force of CT's at only three yards distant. They engaged the enemy hand to hand. During the action Private Jackson had accounted for three CT's when a bullet smashed the breach of his rifle. One man, seeing Jackson at a disadvantage, bayonet charged him. Jackson avoided the thrust and disarmed the man dispatching him with his own bayonet. The enemy raiding party then broke contact and rapidly withdrew pursued by Jackson who threw grenades after them.

Private Jackson showed a total disregard for his own safety and defiance in the face of the enemy far greater than one could reasonably expect from a soldier of such junior rank.

'Impressive Wilf but I don't see it gets us very far.' Lucking paused and rubbed his chin pensively 'my granddad's another cantankerous old soldier but he's well past killing anyone now. He also served in Malaya with the Guards around that time; he was wounded, too.'

Next Sunday Martin Lucking treated his granddad to lunch. 'Why don't you ever talk about your experiences fighting in Malaya granddad, and how you were wounded?'

'There's nowt t' talk about Martin' the old man

squirmed looking uncomfortable 'gettin' shot at's just an occupational hazard for a soldier.'

'Ever heard of a guy called Albert Jackson?'

'Heard of him? I'll say. A right stroppy bugger he was, always in trouble. We was both on the same patrol when he won his medal. That's when I got wounded.'

'Good grief. What happened granddad?'

'It's not important.'

' It could be Granddad Albert's in trouble again.'

'Really?' He hesitated then nodded as if making up is mind. 'Well now, we was just finishing a five day patrol, almost home, we walked slap bang into the bastards. Dunno which side was the more surprised. Anyway, I got hit in the leg early on. I was propped against a tree, a ringside seat you might say. I saw Albert's rifle get hit. Next thing I see 'im braining one of 'em with it, snapped the butt it did.' The old man took a long swig from his pint his eyes misty with recollection 'then a big guy charged Albert. He had an old Jap rifle from world war two with a bloody great bayonet on it.' Granddad paused again, tears brimming. 'We lost two good lads that day.'

Lucking reached across and covered his grandfather's hand sympathetically 'what happened then Granddad?'

'Oh, Albert side stepped the bloke, neat as you like. As he went past Albert chopped him in the throat, the guy went down on all fours choking something 'orrible. Albert picked the guy's rifle up, eyes blazing, screaming like a banshee. Mad as a bag of snakes he was. He rammed the bayonet all the way up the bloke's backside.'

Lucking sat, mouth agape, staring at his Gramps dumbfounded.

***

'It was self defence' Albert Jackson said stubbornly 'excessive use of force my arse. I'm saying no more.'

Albert's lawyer leaned into his ear 'It would be in your best interest, Mr Jackson, to answer these questions.'

A further half hour of getting nowhere passed as Albert opined on the Government, the courts, modern parents and the schools. Strangely, there was no anger in his voice. 'Right, we'll pop you back into a cell whilst we see what's to be done' Redding said at last.

'Nowt to be done lad, I'll be out of here soon enough. I'll have the last laugh, you'll see.'

Redding didn't answer wondering about Albert Jackson's mental state. He was so icy calm, like none of this mattered to him.

Later, a constable took Albert a meal and found the old boy dead.

'Bloody hell' cried Redding when he heard the

news 'why couldn't he have croaked yesterday or waited until we'd bailed him?'

He reported to Lucking 'the old git said he'd have the last laugh Sarge. Death in custody, Christ, I'll be filling in bloody forms 'til retirement.'

Lucking gave a wry smile 'A cantankerous old git indeed.'

Fire Insurance

Elmer towered over his sister-in-law 'you have no goddamned right to this house Jessica' he bawled. He was the only son since his brother David died. Only son and heir, wasn't he? His mother had no right to leave her house, his house, to her. Jessica and her brat had no damned rights at all.

'But, Elmer, it was your mother's last wish and it was me who nursed her for the past fifteen years, after all. Besides, where would we go?' Jessica's lips trembled, her cornflower eyes, wide with fear, looked unnaturally large in her deathly white face. She was glad her Susan was still at school.

Elmer shook from head to toe, incandescent in his rage 'Go? Go?' he screamed, 'you can go to hell for all I care this is my rightful inheritance and I will have it. I'll burn you out if I have to. If I can't have my house, then no one will' veins stood out like bloated worms over his collar and his knuckles showed white as he bunched his fists, 'I'll give you a week to get a lawyer to transfer the property to me and leave. Or else.'

Jessica quaked, but despite being petrified she gathered what remained of her courage for Susan's sake. 'You've never called here once since David's funeral nine years ago Elmer, not once. Nor have you paid a single cent towards the upkeep. When I begged you to look after Mom, so Susan and I could take a short holiday you never answered my letters or returned my calls. You neglected us all for years and now you want to throw us out of our home. You wouldn't dare act like this if my David were still alive. No, no and no again!'

She glared her defiance which quickly turned to fear as he stepped towards her, fist raised, his red face contorted. he towered over his sister-in-law 'you have no goddamned right to this house Jessica' he bawled. He was the only son since his brother David died. Only son and heir, wasn't he? His mother had no right to leave her house, his house, to her. Jessica and her brat had no damned rights at all.

'But, Elmer, it was your mother's last wish and it was me who nursed her for the past fifteen years, after all. Besides, where would we go?' Jessica's lips trembled, her cornflower eyes, wide with fear, looked unnaturally large in her deathly white face. She was glad her Susan was still at school.

Elmer shook from head to toe, incandescent in his rage 'Go? Go?' he screamed, 'you can go to hell for all I care this is my rightful inheritance and I will have it. I'll burn you out if I have to. If I can't have my house, then no one will' veins stood out like bloated worms over his collar and his knuckles showed white as he bunched his fists, 'I'll give you a week to get a lawyer to transfer the property to me and leave. Or else.'

Jessica quaked, but despite being petrified she gathered what remained of her courage for Susan's sake. 'You've never called here once since David's funeral nine years ago Elmer, not once. Nor have you paid a single cent towards the upkeep. When I begged you to look after Mom, so Susan and I could take a short holiday you never answered my letters or returned my calls. You neglected us all for years and now you want to throw us out of our home. You wouldn't dare act like this if my David were still alive. No, no and no again!'

She glared her defiance which quickly turned to fear as he stepped towards her, fist raised, his red face contorted.

'What on earth is going on here? What's all this about burning houses?'

They turned to see Norma Heptonstall, Jessica's neighbour and friend of many years standing in the doorway. 'Is everything OK, Jess?'

Jessica sniffled and hurriedly wiped a tear from her eye. 'Yes, er… yes Norma, my, my brother-in-law is just leaving.'

Elmer realised he'd been overheard making threats and rapidly changed tack. His long, lugubrious face looking slightly less angry as he attempted a weak smile. 'Oh, just a heat of the moment thing,' he mumbled, waving an arm airily, 'like Jess said, I'm just leaving.' He hurried out, throwing a scowl at Jessica as he went.

Norma's brow was furrowed, her mouth turned down at the corners, 'I'm sorry Jess but I couldn't help but overhear, he was very loud. That looked extremely dangerous to me, you should report him.'

Jessica shrugged 'I think he'll calm down now that he's been witnessed making threats. He'll get over it I'm sure.'

'I wouldn't be so certain Jess, houses here on Martha's Vineyard have gone up dramatically over the last twenty years. This place must be worth a couple of million now.'

'Then it's not in his interests to burn it, is it?' Jessica said feeling a little calmer now 'I think he'll realise he's been acting crazy.'

Norma looked dubious, 'you told me he's an obsessive gambler, Jess. People like that can be totally irrational, I'd report him right now if I were you.'

'OK, Norma, but Susan will be home from school any minute and I don't want her to be frightened. I'll report him in the morning.'

Then ten-year-old Susan arrived full of whirligig energy, kisses, tickles, hugs and laughter.

*****

Midnight, the phone rang. Jessica snatched it up quickly so that Susan wouldn't be disturbed.

'Look out the window, Jessica.'

She could see the security light was on above the porch. Drawing back the curtain Jessica saw Elmer standing in the drive holding up a gasoline can in his left hand and a cigarette lighter in his right. His cell phone was trapped between his ear and his shoulder. 'Get outta my house Jess, get out real soon' he said ominously. He turned and walked slowly away, leaving her paralysed with fear.

She put on a housecoat and sat at the picture window looking out, crying softly, until it was time to get Susan up for school. She hadn't rung the police not wanting sirens and flashing lights frightening Susan. With her daughter gone now, Jessica rang and reported Elmer.

'OK, we'll keep an eye out for him and we'll drop by your place on patrol' she was told 'most of these threats come to nothing so don't be too worried ma'am. We'll pick him up for sure if he comes near you.'

The officer sounded far too casual for Jessica's liking; she did not feel reassured.

When Susan came home, she said, 'Hi mom, there was a man outside the school this afternoon, he said to ask if you had fire insurance?'

Jessica's blood ran cold. She sent Susan to her room to do her homework then rang the police again.

No, she did not know where he was staying or what name he was using. She described him as best she could. They listened and said they'd alert all officers to be on the lookout for him. They'd send an officer around the next day to file a report and advise on security. It was tourist season and the small force was overstretched.

Elmer lay deep in the woods his thoughts dark. The house was rightfully his. He'd waited long years for that house to be his. When he sold it, he would pay off all his gambling debts, loans and mortgage arrears leaving enough for a great trip to Las Vegas. He'd be among the high rollers, treated with great respect. His luck would change this time, it always did for high rollers. He'd call again tonight and pour gasoline into the porch, but he wouldn't light it. Just leave it as a message.

Earlier, he'd watched as Susan left for school then he'd approached her at home time. He felt sure that now Jessica knew he'd identified her daughter that it would rack up the pressure. The gasoline threat should seal it. Yes, he'd get the house alright it was just a matter of keeping on racking up the pressure.

Jessica sat sipping green tea to calm her nerves, she could hear Susan up in her room, homework finished, singing at the top of her voice. Her love for Susan hardened her fear into cold anger at Elmer. What right had that waster to threaten them? She started to think of ways to thwart him. After half an hour she had a plan, it was a drastic one, but it could work. She'd been a chemist in the days before she had to give it up to nurse her sick mother-in-law, she had skills she could use.

She looked in the medicine cupboard. The old lady had believed in old-fashioned remedies. Yes, there it was, a

jar of potassium permanganate. She took it and went to the kitchen where she found the other ingredient she needed.

The porch door stuck, it had always dragged across the wooden floor the first four inches. It was one of those minor jobs she'd get around to fixing one day. She mixed a small batch and placed it carefully. She opened the door, it made its usual protest as it rubbed hard over the uneven flooring. Yes, yes! It worked as she'd hoped.

Jessica rang Norma and asked if she and Susan could stay over that night in case Elmer came back. Norma happily obliged.

Jessica sent Susan over to Norma's house then went to the garden shed and found the can of gas for the lawnmower. She took an old plastic washbowl and filled it. After she'd completed her arrangements, she packed an overnight bag and went to join Susan and Norma. Of her plan, she said nothing.

When officer John Bradwell swung by the house at 2 a.m. All was quiet, the house in darkness. He shone his powerful torch around the garden. Everything looked to be in order. He reported in then carried on with his patrol.

Elmer watched him go then sneaked out of his hiding place in the bushes and crept up the side of the house avoiding the security light's sensor. After a final look around, he unscrewed the cap of his fuel can and pushed the porch door. It stuck so he pushed again, impatiently.

The compound that Jessica had put on the scrape area on the floor burst into flames as the grinding door caused friction. The washbowl she'd balanced above cascaded its lethal liquid over Elmer and into the flames.

Jessica and her neighbours came running on hearing Elmer's agonised shrieks. They found him writhing on the lawn engulfed in flames. They eventually managed to beat him out. They also managed to contain the porch fire, too, as flashing lights and wailing sirens approached. The house was saved. Elmer was not.

Jessica looked at the smouldering corpse dispassionately 'Yes, Elmer,' she whispered, 'I've got fire insurance.'

A Hollow Promise

As we kissed passionately, my hand slid up her slender thigh.

'Ouch!'

I was shocked 'you're still a virgin?'

She blushed 'yes. But...but I don't mind, really...' she sounded far from certain.

Amrita was a slim, alluring Indian girl of twenty with huge molten eyes and shining coal-black hair that smelled subtlety of jasmine. Her figure was divine. I'd met her a few days earlier whilst I was on a routine patrol.

We caught some rioters red-handed about to torch her father's shop. Amrita was bravely confronting two large men with a walking stick. The men were sneering at her pretending to be frightened. Amrita's terrified father was trying to block his shop doorway.

We applied a little rifle butt diplomacy, persuading the rioters not to bother. We arrested the ringleader and the rest suddenly remembered urgent appointments elsewhere. Amrita's father was overjoyed, so was she; that modest little shop was not only their livelihood but also their home. As my patrol leader took her father's statement, I chatted her up.

Now, we were lying on a blanket in a hollow in the deserted sandy beach, it was late afternoon, the sun's power was fading as it arced into the far horizon. The sea was a rich chocolate brown, turbid with the outpouring mud from the Demerara River. Over the sea wall that towered above us and to our right, the bandstand's leaden roof shone dully. The breeze made a soft, soughing sound as it carried the call of the Kiskadees from the distant trees. Kiskadee, kiskadee, kisk, kisk, kiskadee they called as they squabbled over nesting rights. Overhead a toucan flew its huge bill balanced before it. It felt like we were the only two people in the world.

We kissed again then I rolled away and lit a cigarette, propping myself on one elbow. I had to cool down. I switched on my portable radio The Drifters were singing Under the Boardwalk. It was a favourite of mine, Amrita loved it, too.

She was silent as she watched me from under her long eyelashes, face cast down. Her full lips trembled with anxiety as her hand unconsciously pushed her dress kneewards.

In British Guiana* 1964 'nice' girls came on a first date with a chaperone (You'd better believe it) otherwise it was assumed all systems go. I felt bad. She'd trusted me without a maiden aunt's presence and I'd pushed it too far. I backed off, 'Sorry

Amrita,' I said, I thought…… '

'Don't you find me attractive?' She asked, her voice trembling.

'Yes, of course I do, but you're not certain and I could get into big trouble for pushing you. You have to be certain Amrita and I don't think you are, are you?'

'I... I think I am Tony' she said,

Think you are? God! Not good enough I thought. We soldiers had to be so damn careful. We couldn't afford to give anyone a reason to cry rape. We were there to keep the peace so had to maintain a high level of discipline. At present, both sides of the racial divide trusted us, but it was a tricky balancing act. The people of African descent and the people of Indian descent were many and we were few. The consequences of alienating either community didn't bear thinking about. All the racists on either side wanted to do was kill each other; we didn't want them to include us.

When we weren't patrolling, we mended bridges, repaired schools, played football and cricket with both sides. The usual hearts and minds stuff.

Amrita felt very special to me from the moment I first saw her bravely facing the rioters despite her obvious fear. I was smitten. Contrary to popular belief, we soldiers were not all 'wham, bam, thank you, ma'am.'

I stubbed out my cigarette and took her in my

arms. She was so slender, so light she felt like a beautiful, fragile doll. We kissed, and I felt her relax as she realised I was not going to force myself on her. I didn't want her to do it out of a sense of gratitude because we'd saved their shop.

Our first date over, we agreed to meet in two days' time, it would be my first full day off in a month. Eager with anticipation we parted on a kiss and a promise.

Two days later things went tits up as a building was blown up downtown. All days off were cancelled. We spent the day searching rubble, looking for bodies and parts thereof whilst keeping rubberneckers at bay. By the time we got back to the corrugated iron cricket pavilion we called home we were knackered. I fell on my camp bed and slept until ten that night. Amrita had been and gone.

Next night, in Laddie's bar, after drinking more stress reliever than was good for me, I fell for the charms of a bar girl we called Nellie-the-Belly. When she performed her belly dance, Nellie commanded the full attention of every bloke with a pulse. Amrita came into the bar and saw Nellie on my knee. Her face fell, and she turned and hurried away. By the time I'd untangled myself and gone after her, she was nowhere to be seen. I was mortified.

I persuaded our patrol leader to call at her shop next day, but her father said she'd gone away to visit relatives. I didn't believe him, but we had a job to do and couldn't hang around.

On my next afternoon off, I was again laying in the hollow hoping against hope that Amrita would somehow turn up, but it had been ten days since she fled. The Kiskadees were still clashing and the same soft warm wind blew over the muddy sea. I was reading a book written by a Canadian bloke who'd been successfully sluicing the rivers of Guiana for alluvial gold and diamonds. He described how, on a break from prospecting, he was lying in a hollow on the Georgetown beach with the bandstand roof a little way to his right over the seawall. He and his girl had enjoyed a little 'afternoon delight.' Ironically, I was reading this lying in that very same hollow.

My heart ached for Amrita and what might have been. I remembered the moment I first saw her and how my heart had lurched. I'd gingerly asked for a date and couldn't believe my luck when she said yes.

But now I had to be practical. I was a common soldier for God's sake, with bugger-all to offer. The year before we'd been fighting the Indonesians in the jungles of Borneo, now we were here trying to keep the peace. Who knew what hell-hole they'd send us to next time? What right had I to hope? To even dream? You're a bloody fool I told myself, you brought it on your own head and you deserve your sorry arse kicking. Then Under the Boardwalk came on my radio and I confess to being unsoldierly enough to shed a tear.

Postscript: Nellie-the-Belly moved on to her next conquest the moment my pay was spent. Shortly after that we were gone, shouted upriver to quell yet another troublesome piss hole. I never saw my virgin again.

*Now named Guyana since independence in 1966

Kindness is its Own Reward

Pamela Prentice saw the elderly gentleman stagger and fall. He seemed to be stepping up the kerb and somehow toppled over his ankle twisting under him. He landed heavily bumping his head as he sprawled across the pavement. She stopped her car immediately and ran over to where he lay dazed and bleeding from the head.

'Lie still' she ordered in her authoritative nurse's voice.

'I'll be all right, I'll be all right' he mumbled trying to get up.

'Please let be the judge of that,' she said gently 'I'm a trained nurse I can help you' and, ignoring his protestations, proceeded to examine him. He sensed from her actions and questions that she knew what she was about and relaxed a little letting her tend to him.

A woman came out of her house to offer help 'I've called an ambulance' she said, 'but they said there's a delay.'

Pamela looked resigned there was often a delay these days in getting to minor incidents. Ah well, she thought I'd better take him myself. Between them, the two women got the casualty into her car where he sat on the back seat looking bemused and forlorn holding a napkin to his bleeding head.

'If you just drop me off at home, I'll be OK' he said, 'I don't want to be a bother.'

Pamela looked at him through the rear-view mirror 'I believe you've broken your ankle young man' she said sounding school ma'am-ish 'You'll need professional attention for that' and with that, she drove him to the Accident and Emergency department of the local hospital.

Pamela had asked him his name and established that he lived alone during her examination so there was no one she could call for him. She booked him in then handed him over to a hospital porter who wheeled him away for treatment then she left to go shopping.

Peter Lovage received excellent treatment his broken ankle was put in a cast and, because he'd banged his head, he was kept in hospital overnight for observation. On his release, he took a taxi home and with the help of the driver and his new crutches managed to get into his house without too much trouble. The hospital had informed the social services people who said they'd send someone round to assess his needs.

Pamela told her husband John about what had happened and how she was concerned for the eighty-one-year-old gentleman. When she said she was going to pop around after work the next day to see if he was all right John was not surprised. That was his Pamela, a heart of gold, always looking out for others. He knew better than to argue, she'd take no notice anyway.

And so it was Pamela knocked on Peter's door and heard him call 'Come in the door's open.' He looked surprised to see her 'oh it's you, I thought it was the social services lady. Well, I'm glad you've called m'dear because I wanted to thank you for your help the other day. It was very kind of you.'

Peter offered to pay her for the petrol used but she refused him briskly. 'No thank you' she said: 'my mother always taught us that kindness should be its own reward.' He looked thin and frail with a sort of lost look about him 'When did you last eat?'

He paused rubbing his chin as if trying to think of the answer to a difficult question 'this morning, yes, yes definitely, I made some toast....' his voice trailed off and then he followed with 'I'm fine, really I can manage.'

Pamela looked at him sternly 'Well I'm going to make you a cup of tea while I'm here and see what else I can do.'

In the kitchen, she found everything clean and well-ordered like the rest of the small terraced house appeared to be. On opening the fridge, though, there wasn't much in the way of food. She managed to make him a cheese omelette and opened a tin of peas to go with it, taking it through on a tray along with a cup of tea for them both.

'Right, Peter, you eat this now and we'll have a cup of tea then see what's to be done about shopping, you don't seem to have much food in the house.'

'I was on my way to the shops when I fell', he said defensively 'I don't eat a great lot anyway.'

There and then Pamela took out a pen and her notebook 'I'll get you something in, what do you normally eat?' Her tone told him it was no use arguing so he reeled off a short list. Pamela thought no wonder he looks so thin he's not eating properly. After a few suggestions from her, the list filled out a little and she went and got what she thought would last him for a week. On her return, they chatted for a little while and that's when Pamela first noticed the photograph in the silver frame on the mantelpiece. It was of a young pretty woman with flame red hair smiling broadly she was stood in a relaxed pose holding the hand of a little girl of about three. What aroused her curiosity was the narrow band of black ribbon tied around the top. Not wanting to pry she said nothing but Peter had noticed her looking.

Pamela called the following morning before her shift and found that Peter was up and about. She could smell the bacon and toast he'd made for breakfast. He seemed much recovered in his spirits and insisted on making her coffee. 'It's proper coffee

Pamela not that instant stuff' he said as if to reassure her.

Pamela was pleased, one of her little weaknesses was proper ground coffee and she'd skipped hers that morning in order to spend a bit more time with him 'Oh well, in that case, you've persuaded me' she beamed 'no sugar or milk for me please.'

'That's the way I drink it too' he said seeming pleased at her revelation.

Over the weeks of Peter's recovery, he and Pamela became good friends. She discovered he had a dry, wicked sense of humour and a keen wit, he always seemed to look for the good in people too and she liked that about him. They also shared a love of poetry although their tastes varied widely.

He told her he'd been an engineer and had worked all over the world. They reminisced fondly of Singapore where Pamela had spent three years as a teenager due to her father's work.

Peter made her laugh with funny stories too like the time when in a small town in Malaysia he had been staying in a guest house and had indulged in rather too much whiskey. On returning to his room he had found a huge snake asleep on his bed. Annoyed he had grabbed the reptile behind its head and thrown it out of the window. When he told the manager the next morning the man went pale. Peter had thought because of its size that the snake was a non-poisonous python, but the manager told him what he had just described was a king cobra, the world's largest poisonous snake. The nearest anti-venom serum he said was in Kuala Lumpur seventy-five miles away.

When the conversation turned to family matters Peter was reluctant to talk of any relatives he may have had and quickly changed the subject. Pamela was still fascinated by the photo on the mantelpiece, but he never mentioned it as she sensed it was a bit of a taboo subject so, although intrigued, good manners prevented her from asking.

Over that summer Peter came to Pamela and John's house for a barbeque and to Sunday lunch a few times. He met their ten-year-old daughter Molly. He and Molly had hit it off straight away 'It's like having another granddad,' she told her mother 'he's so funny, always telling me silly jokes.'

One day whilst having tea at Peter's house they had been talking about Molly who had been excited about a forthcoming sleepover at her cousin's house. Pamela finally broached the subject of his family; did he have anyone at all like a distant cousin for instance? Had he ever been married?

Peter was quiet for a moment then got out of his chair and handed her the photo from the mantelpiece 'We were married' he stated, 'She died.'

'Oh, I'm sorry Peter and the little girl? Is she your daughter?'

He paused and took the picture from her looking

at it wistfully stroking it gently with the tips of his fingers as if caressing them both 'Yes, she was my daughter' he said his voice quiet. His eyes filled with sadness 'she died, too.'

Pamela wished now she hadn't asked she could see he was hurting. 'Sorry, Peter....I didn't mean to cause you pain. Was it an accident?'

'In a way' he paused, she was an Irish girl you see, from Londonderry. She went to visit her sister whilst I was away on a job, 1972 it was. I asked her not to go as she was eight months pregnant but she was a headstrong girl, my Colleen. He paused again as if struggling to find the right words finally he said simply 'they were out shopping, looking for a present for me' again, he hesitated briefly shrugging his shoulders 'there was a bomb.'

His words hit Pamela like a blow to the jaw, she felt sick in the pit of her stomach. He had stated 'there was a bomb' with no trace of self-pity, no bitterness, no hatred of the people who had planted the device, no hint of any emotion.

'Oh, Peter I'm so sorry. Oh, my God, that's awful and your unborn child and your little girl too...' she broke off sobbing.

Peter placed his hand on her shoulder 'It was all such a long time ago now my dear and I've forgiven them, please, don't upset yourself.'

Pamela wiped the tears from her eyes and blew into her handkerchief. 'Your daughter, she looks so beautiful, what was she called?'

'Molly' he said quietly, replacing the picture 'she was called Molly, just like your little girl.'

Peter spared her the details of those terrible times. There had been a warning, but they got the street name wrong and the bomb had gone off twenty minutes early as people were still being evacuated past the empty shop where the device lay hidden.

Heavily pregnant and hampered with shopping Colleen and Molly had been the last people struggling to clear the area. They were blown through a shop window and Colleen and her unborn child died instantly. Her body had partially shielded Molly from the blast. She was found among the rubble unconscious, her left foot severed completely, blood seeping from her nose and ears. Molly looked like a beautiful broken doll.

They had tried so hard to save her. Peter had sat by her bed for three days and nights in the intensive care ward praying for her, holding her hand, willing her to live.

On the morning of the fourth day, she had opened her bright blue eyes and recognised her daddy. She couldn't smile for the tube in her throat, but her eyes lit up with joy at seeing him. He had told her he loved her and that he was asking God to make her better.

Shortly afterwards she had slipped into a coma and two hours later her brave spirit gave up the impossible struggle to stay in her shattered little body. She let out a last short sighing breath and passed away. Peter never prayed again.

It was winter time and Pamela was concerned for Peter he'd had a bad cold since Christmas which had turned into a nasty chest infection. He had taken the medicine she had got for him and the doctor had visited, prescribing antibiotics. Peter had seemed to be rallying well but, as always, he looked so terribly frail.

Three days after the doctor had been Pamela found him dead in bed his heart had failed under the strain. He looked so at peace like a man who had finally arrived home to his loved ones after a long, tiring journey.

Pamela and John arranged his funeral and had been the only mourners. Pamela had cried tears of genuine grief at his passing for she had grown to love the beautiful person he was. Molly was too distraught to attend and had stayed with her grandparents.

Two weeks later they received a call from a solicitor would they please come to the office for the reading of the will. Pamela had been surprised as she hadn't known he even had a will; they had never discussed anything to do with financial matters. She knew he owned his house but had assumed that the proceeds of the sale would go to the state seeing as he had no living relatives.

They came away from the lawyers in a state of shock and walked in silence to their car. After what seemed an eternity Pamela spoke 'Good grief John' she muttered, still unable to believe what the solicitor had told them. 'I had absolutely no idea. I mean, his house and seven rental properties for us and three hundred and forty-eight thousand pounds in trust for Molly?'

John started the engine 'Your mother was right about kindness it seems.'

Confucius, He Say...

(A tale from ancient China)

The palankeen bearers were sweating profusely as they set down the two old friends at the public bathhouse. As they crossed to the entrance an old peasant stumbled on the uneven paving and almost fell into one of the grand gentlemen.

'Out of the way dog, how dare you bar my path?' Nee Sun was outraged and pushed the old fellow who, being already off balance, fell heavily to the ground before them.

The man rolled away then scrambled to his knees knocking his forehead three times on the ground in grovelling apology. Nee Sun turned away in disgust, but his companion Chee Yang stooped and helped the old fellow to his feet. He had a heavy grey beard and his long, dishevelled hair was matted around his face.

'When did you last eat old fellow?'

'Just two days ago sir' he said with head downcast not daring to look such a great gentleman in the face.

Reaching into the sleeve of his magnificent silk

robe Chee Yang extracted a string of fifty coppers which he pressed on the peasant. The old man cried out in gratitude and bowed deeply then scuttled off singing Chee Yang's praises.

Nothing was said until after the bath and the men were in the steam room away from the attendants then Nee Sun said puzzled 'why did you soil your hands on that lowly dog and give him fifty cash when he had offended us?'

'What offence did he commit brother?'

'You saw him bar our path, the clumsy oaf.'

'And what if one of us had stumbled and barred his path?'

'What in heaven's name do you mean Chee Yang? We are vastly superior to that lowly dog.'

'Oh, we are? In what way?'

Nee Sun's eyebrows arched almost into his hairline 'how many ships do you own Chee Yang? How many godowns are full of your goods?'

'I have one hundred and forty-two trading junks and seven godowns as you well know Nee Sun two ships fewer than you as you are always at pains to remind me.'

'Well, there you are then my strange friend. You are a wealthy merchant, the son of a wealthy merchant, educated, cultured and vastly superior to that low dog in every way.'

'No sir, I am richer and more privileged than he, true, and heaven has smiled upon my fortune but in what way am I his superior?'

Nee Sun stared wide eyed at his friend, speechless. Chee had always been a strange fellow but since he had started studying Confucius two years ago, he had become even more strange. Nee shook his head in silent bewilderment.

'You see, Nee Sun, these poor fellows have no wealth. They go out daily to labour for a few coppers lest their families starve. They live in hovels you and I would not keep our dogs in. Yet love for their wives and children keep them going out day after day pulling carts, carrying our palankeens or emptying our shit pots with so little reward and no hope of improvement. Could you do it?

'Could you Chee Yang?'

Chee Yang paused as if considering the question. 'Do you remember last month I told you I was making a trip? I was absent for a week.

'Ah yes, visiting your esteemed brother the magistrate in the next province.'

'My humble apologies brother Sun that was a lie.'

'Really?'

'I disguised myself as a peasant, lived in a cheap hostel and found work as a labourer when I could.'

'By the gods whatever for man?'

'To learn humility and to show penitence for my former arrogance; It was a hard lesson working in one of your godowns Sun. I was set to carrying heavy bales from dawn until dusk without a break just to earn enough for my lodgings and a bowl of noodles.'

'But you have a mansion, four wives and the gods only know how many concubines and an army of servant's brother Yang, and yet you would you debase yourself so, why?'

'Do you remember Wen Po?'

'Yes, he lost his fortune gambling then killed himself; can't say I blame the fellow.'

'And now his wives and children are destitute and living on the mercy of relatives. He was a young well-educated man. I offered him work as an administrator in my business, but he turned me down saying that such work was beneath the dignity of a gentleman.'

'It is often the case with us the superior classes.'

'Sadly, yes, and yet in honest work, I found no indignity, quite the opposite in fact.' Chee Yang tugged his long moustache pensively, 'Wen Po chose death to preserve his pride over the wellbeing of his family. How then was he superior to that poor fellow who fell before us?'

Nee Sun was embarrassed, he had no answer, so he changed the subject. 'Are you going to the Governor's feast tonight Chee Yang?'

'Yes, as a fellow Confucian His Excellency was gracious enough to invite me, doubtless I will see you there.'

'I suppose you are after the contract to carry the army's supplies on your fleet, Yang?'

'Yes, Sun, I have put in a bid, as I know you have.'

'Of course, Yang, and I shall win, too. Just you wait and see.'

Chee Yang had long suspected that his friend used bribes to gain lucrative Government contracts, a crime punishable by death if caught. 'Perhaps you will my friend, personally, I prefer not to risk my head.' Nee Sun gave a sour look but said nothing.

The feast in the Governor's palace was a splendid occasion lit with hundreds of bright lampions. There were dancers and acrobats to entertain the guests and the finest food and wines were served. As the banquet ended, the Governor called the two friends to his dais.

Both men bowed low before the Governor, 'I have decided to award the army contract of transport to the honourable Chee Yang' he said imperiously.

Both men bowed deeply again in acceptance. As they did so Chee Yang saw a look of bitter disappointment cross his friend's face. The decision of the Provincial Governor was as final as that of the emperor himself; there could be no further negotiation.

At the end of the feast, His Excellency was saying farewell to each guest individually as was his custom. When Nee Sun's turn came, he offered profuse thanks for the evening's feast, bowing low before this personal representative of the August Emperor himself. As he bowed, he noticed a wound on the governor's wrist. 'You are injured, Your Excellency, I shall send my personal physician in the morning to attend you.' Nee Sun said obsequiously, 'How could your Highness have come by such a wound?'

'You are too kind Nee Sun, but the wound is of little consequence I, clumsy fellow that I am, stumbled and fell this morning outside the public baths.'

Weasel Words

Sometimes a drastic situation requires thinking outside the box.

'Honestly Granddad I'm at my wit's end, they were at it again last night until four this morning. I don't know how much longer I can go on.' Jenny sniffed and wiped a tear from her eye. 'They have rap music blaring night and day and their language is disgusting. Little Billy is terrified of playing in the garden, yesterday they threw a big slab of concrete over the fence, it could have killed him if it had hit him.'

The final straw had been when Jenny came home from her part-time job that afternoon to find that an obscenity had been scrawled across her window in human excrement.

Mick looked serious, his normally smooth brow was knit in a deep frown he hated to see his granddaughter like this. It was the third time this month she'd come over to ask if she and Billy his three-year-old grandson could stay the night. Her neighbours, a family called Witzell, known locally as the Weasels, were one of the county's worst antisocial problem families. They seemed to revel in antagonizing their neighbours, appearing in court and being the local press.

The 'Weasel' family consisted of Alice Witzell the matriarch her husband Jock a giant of a man who came and went as he pleased between his home and that of his pregnant lover, two sons Keylon and Jago aged sixteen and eighteen respectively their fourteen-year-old sister Jaynie-Shannon completed the household.

Keylon and Jago rode around the district on a noisy motorcycle or sat on it in the garden revving the engine for what seemed like hours at a time. They partied most nights getting drunk and fighting and on more than one occasion they had urinated through Jenny's letterbox. Jaynie-Shannon delighted in screeching obscenities at Jenny every time she saw her in her garden.

True the local authorities had threatened to evict them but that was a long process the threat of which served only to goad the Witzells on to even more outrageous behaviour. Lately, they had bought a large fierce looking dog which, with some predictability, they had named Tyson. The animal spent its time chained in the garden barking when the lads were not parading it around the streets showing it off and intimidating folk. It seemed there was no one who had the courage to stand up to this family from hell, or was there?

If Jenny protested to the Witzells they only

sneered at her, if she called the police, they threatened her and her son. As a single mother, Jenny felt isolated, trapped with no one to turn to. The police had other priorities and were too slow to respond effectively, the other so-called 'Authorities' had had a word with the Witzells on numerous occasions; the Social Services were mostly too scared to call and when the local council people did eventually call to 'gather evidence' as they put it, they came at nine thirty in the morning when all was quiet because the Witzell's were still in bed nursing hangovers.

To Jenny and her neighbours, it seemed that all they got was the run around 'We're doing our best Ms Hartnell, it's difficult to find appropriate accommodation for these families Ms Hartnell, blah, blah bloody blah Ms Hartnell...'

Jenny went upstairs and prepared the spare room for her and Billy. Why she told granddad Mick her woes she didn't know, he was an old man for goodness sake. Well, sixty-eight was old in her eyes, what on earth could he do about it a gentle old soul like him? She couldn't tell her parents as they would simply advise her to forgive them and pray to the lord for a solution.

Granddad Mick was a widower and a good listener whom she adored so it was he, poor fellow, who was her shoulder to cry on.

Mick was as fit and active as a man of his age

could be. He went swimming three or four times a week and walked everywhere weather permitting, he also had a very keen intelligence coupled with a readiness to act when required. Although on the surface he was sweet-natured, harmless older gentleman he was also a man who got things done and now as he sat deep in thought, an idea was forming in his mind that might just fit the bill.

Jenny finished preparing the room and went downstairs. 'I'm going to pick Billy up from the nursery school now gramps can I make you a brew before I go?'

'No love I'm fine you get on.'

As soon as she had left the house, Mick went out to his garden shed 'Hmmnn now let me see' he mused to himself. Oh yes, he thought, I'll need to buy some of that and one of those. After rummaging around for ten minutes he'd finally assembled a small, diverse collection of articles. There was a small wooden stake, a funnel, some fishing line and a roll of gaffer tape which he stuffed into an old haversack he then locked the shed, checked his watch and saw he still had time to do a little research online before his granddaughter returned.

That evening with Billy bathed and put to bed Mick poured them both a drink and they settled into comfortable armchairs but instead of putting the television on Mick said he had something to tell her.

'Jenny, I think I have a solution to your problem,

it's one I cannot divulge just now 'cos I'm still finalising the details, but I want you to stop worrying.'

Jenny looked dubious 'What on earth are you talking about gramps? You can't possibly take on the Witzells at your age.'

'Who said I was going to?' he queried, a sly look in his eye. 'All I'm going to do is write them a note, a few words of advice you might say.'

Jenny's jaw dropped she stared at him as though he'd taken leave of his senses. 'A note'? She asked incredulously 'what the hell good do you think note will do Gramps?'

'Ah, well,' Mick said conspiratorially 'This will be a very special note, one that commands attention and will be taken seriously and that's all I'm saying on the subject.'

'Like hell, you are gramps' Jenny almost shouted 'I want you to promise me you'll not do anything hare-brained or put yourself in danger.' She looked at him through narrowed eyes she knew, gentle creature that he was, he could be as stubborn as a mule and impossible to move once his mind was made up. 'Just promise me you'll not approach them will you gramps? I couldn't stand it if anything bad were to happen to you.'

'I promise darling girl now I'm off to bed for an early night I have a busy day tomorrow.'

Four days later Mick's preparations were

complete, he got into his car with the small rucksack and drove the three miles to park about a mile from his destination where he left the car in a quiet cul-de-sac, donned a wide-brimmed hat to shield his face from street cameras and walked to his granddaughter's house. He didn't stop but walked slowly past on the opposite side of the street glancing at the Witzell's house, taking in the details he would need. From the back of the house, he could hear Tyson barking at nothing in particular. On what passed for a front garden Keylon and Jago were kicking a football about whilst through the open front door came the blare of gangsta rap.

At five thirty the following morning Mick crept down the side of Jenny's house in the first glimmer of dawn and into her back garden. Over the broken fence Tyson started barking as Mick threw the dog a piece of meat he had prepared for the occasion. It was nothing lethal just enough to put the dog to sleep for a few hours.

Mick waited until the animal had succumbed to the sedative then crept silently to the front door where he lifted the flap on the letterbox and made his delivery. After that swift action, he pushed an envelope half though with a surgically gloved hand then moved into the front garden where he crouched down some four yards from the house and busied himself. Less than two minutes later he was making his way home job done.

At seven thirty a.m. Alice Witzell awoke with the feeling that something was not right, she didn't know what it was, but something had disturbed her slumber at what was, for her, an ungodly hour. She scratched her tousled head for a minute slowly gaining a higher level of consciousness; something was definitely wrong.

Climbing out of bed she donned a grubby housecoat and a pair of slippers and went to the bedroom door. It was upon opening the door that the smell hit her it was at once familiar, but she couldn't quite put a name to it. The rest of the house was quiet save for the snoring coming from the boys' bedroom. She checked her daughter's bedroom; the girl was sound asleep.

Feeling uneasy she made her way slowly downstairs her unease growing with every step she took, the smell getting stronger and stronger.

At the bottom, she saw the white envelope sticking through the letterbox. As she went to retrieve it, she, at last, recognised the smell, it was paraffin. As it soaked into her slippers wetting her feet Alice let out a strangled squawk and leapt out of the slippers and ran into the living room. Once in there she tore open the envelope and took out the single sheet of neatly typed paper. Her finger followed the words and her lips moved as she slowly read:

Dear problem family,

We who live around here are at the end of our patience with you and will tolerate no more of your vile behaviour. This paraffin could have been lit with devastating results for all your family. It was not lit on this occasion as it was meant to give you fair warning. This is the only warning you will get. You will from now on behave in a civilised manner, get rid of the dog and show consideration for your neighbours or you can move out, the choice is yours.

Alice's hands shook as she realised the full implication of the threat. She dropped the letter and ran upstairs screaming for the children to wake up. Dashing into her daughter's room she shook her awake then ran into the boys' room still screaming hysterically. The lads were not best pleased with being disturbed and started cursing her.

When they had calmed their mother down enough to discover what had happened Jago, with the stupidity and bravado of immature youth, threw on his jeans and ran downstairs shouting about showing these bastards who was boss around here. As he tore open the front door the fishing line Mick had attached to the door knocker pulled tautly and detonated the large industrial firework he had tied to a stake in the garden. There was a bright flash and an almighty bang that blew out two windows of the Witzell's house.

The ashen-faced youth leapt back into the house and dived behind the sofa screaming for his mother, meanwhile the terrified Jaynie-Shannon cowered under her bed trembling and whimpering losing control of her bladder. Keylon had run out of the back door to fetch Tyson for reasons he alone knew only to find the animal sleeping peacefully and could not be aroused.

The long-suffering neighbours, Jenny included, thinking the bang was just another episode of anti-social behaviour on the part of the Weasels didn't even bother calling the police but, after looking through their curtains for a moment, went back to their slumbers, after all, it was Sunday morning.

Later that day Mick's phone rang 'Granddad you'll never guess what's happened?' Jenny sounded overjoyed 'Mrs Witzell said good morning to me today and actually smiled. A little while later she came to the door and said they were moving out today and staying with relatives 'til they found somewhere else to live.' Jenny gasped, overcome with joy 'would you believe she asked me to keep an eye on their house until they could arrange for their stuff to be moved?

'Oh, good' said Mick grinning widely, 'that is wonderful news, I wonder why they suddenly decided to move?'

'It must have been the power of prayer Gramps, so whatever you were planning doesn't matter now;

mum and dad were right all along about praying.' she laughed 'a letter wouldn't have worked anyway, you silly man.'

Mick smiled sweetly, his face radiating the innocence of the elderly 'Yes, my darling, you're probably right' he said.

Cold Caller

Mrs Mary Lamb lifted the receiver. Her hand shook nervously as apprehension engulfed her. Slowly, her breath quickening, she raised the receiver to her ear. Her old-fashioned phone had no caller I.D. and her daughter's call was long overdue, yet….yet...

'Hello?' she whispered hopefully.

'Good evening madam, may I speak to Mr Gerald Lamb, please?'

Her heart sank. It was yet another one of 'those' calls. Oh, dear, she thought whatever am I to do?

'I'm sorry, I'm afraid my husband passed away six months ago.'

'Oh dear, I'm sorry to hear that Mrs Lamb, perhaps you might be able to help me?'

'What is it about?'

'I'm Jonas Flint, Mrs Lamb, calling on behalf of the charity Aid for Elderly Animals. Your husband was kind enough to help us with a generous donation in the past.'

The smooth, practised voice of the cold caller went on hypnotically, perfect in rhythm, speed, volume and pitch, 'in fact, he indicated that he would be willing to set up a direct debit for a regular amount each month.'

Eighty-six-year-old Mary dreaded these cold calls, this was the third one this week. She felt intimidated, but she was from the old school of good manners and politeness. Mary found it impossible to hang up on cold callers.

'Well, I don't know about that, he was a generous man, that's true, Mr Flint, but we lived in very modest circumstances. We really couldn't afford much, and I have even less now he's gone.'

'Do you have any pets yourself, Mrs Lamb?'

'Oh yes, I've still got Dolly, our little Cavalier King Charles, we've had her a long time now, Mr Flint.'

'Please call me Jonas Mrs Lamb,' his voice professionally friendly, 'So much nicer.'

'Oh, very well, Mr ..er, sorry, Jonas. '

'Thank you. May I call you Mary? It's so much friendlier, don't you think?' He went on without waiting for her consent. 'Let me ask you, Mary if anything were to happen to you, what arrangements have you made for your precious Dolly?'

Mary was confused, she hadn't given the matter any thought, she was still mourning the loss of her late husband 'arrangements? Well, ...er I don't really know, Jonas.'

'Oh, dear Mary, that is bad news' he paused for dramatic effect 'it probably won't matter if Dolly is very old of course, but a lot of pets, especially the old ones that can't be re-homed, are simply put down when anything happens to their owners. That would be awful, wouldn't it?'

'Oh, oh I see, yes, that would be terrible' said Mary her hand-wringing the handset, her knuckles white. She was scared and emotional now. She looked at the elderly Dolly sleeping peacefully at her feet and her heart filled with love and fear.

Flint pressed on 'we at Aid for Elderly Animals, give a home to these pets Mary and guarantee that they are looked after until such time as they join their owners again in the hereafter. All we ask for Mary is say, twenty pounds to help us to carry on this important work on behalf of these poor bereaved pets.'

'Yes, I see' she said, but I already have twelve charity direct debits, Jonas, I really can't afford another, honestly.'

'Well, how about a smaller amount then Mary, say ten? And perhaps a modest donation now, say another ten? That would carry us over until the direct debit started Mary.' When she hesitated, he continued 'surely, ten pounds is not an unreasonable amount to ensure the future wellbeing of your precious Dolly? It's such a worthy cause, and you'd be a vital part of helping other unfortunate animals, too. Have you got your card to hand, Mary?'

He was then silent. Silence, he knew, builds like a pressure cooker; the question hangs there,

demanding an answer, creating a force of its own. The mind struggles, trying to find an adequate reason or excuse. It nearly always fails in that dreadful vacuum of the deadly silence. Flint called it the embarrassment factor, it was a pressure tactic he used successfully every day.

Mary looked down at Dolly again and caved in, reaching for her handbag, her heart palpitating, feeling confused and emotional. She gave her details. Ten pounds would leave her very short and her pension wasn't due for another week.

Flint put down the phone, it was break time. He looked at the man in the next booth and slapped him on the back. 'Coming for a snack, Henry?'

Henry shook his head 'I've not reached my target yet Jonas, I still need another three.'

Flint smirked 'I've told you before mate, you're too bloody soft on them; play to their emotions, sing to their souls, it works every time.'

Henry said, 'I heard you telling that woman that we look after old dogs until the end of their days Jonas, but we euthanise all those too old to be rehomed, you know that.'

Yeah, right, but she doesn't know that, does she?

'But that's not ethical, Jonas.'

'You can't spend ethics mate' Flint replied callously 'look, let me show you something, Henry' he glanced down at Mrs Lamb's details. 'Take this old biddy, she says her old man has croaked, that's a standard defence some of these folks put up. It may or may not be true. Ignore it. Next, she says she's got loads of direct debits. She thinks that will put me off. No way! She's just told me she's vulnerable, a sucker, right? She's done it before, so she'll do it again. Take no notice of poverty pleas or you'll never make any bonus.' He looked at Henry, his hard eyes reflecting his name. 'Keep on going mate, find their weak spot and go in for the kill. They've all got money mate, there's no reason for them not to give.'

Henry thought of his own grandparents, they didn't have much money. They got cold calls too, but his granddad was an ex-Sergeant Major who dealt with them crisply.

'What if they're genuine Jonas and really are broke?'

'Then they'll cancel their direct debit mate, but if you activate it immediately, then you'll have the first month's payment and the donation.'

He placed a hand on Henry's arm, his smile not reaching his eyes. Flint liked to feel important, to demonstrate his superior techniques 'now, take Mrs Lamb-to-the-slaughter here, she's scared stiff her dog will outlive her. I spun her the yarn about us looking after her pet when she's gone, right? Boom, ten quid just like that and a direct debit for ten, too. That was just my foot in her door. I'll ring her next month to up the DD and press her for another donation.'

Flint looked down at her details again 'Well,

bless my soul' he said laughing 'I didn't notice that before, it says here, husband's occupation: Healer and white witch.' Flint guffawed, 'I tell you mate, these people are all full of shit.' He went to his break, still smiling.

Mrs Lamb looked at the cash machine screen, her balance was eight pounds twenty-seven pence. The minimum withdrawal was ten pounds. Aid for Elderly Animals had taken her ten pounds donation and activated her direct debit simultaneously. She had not expected that, thinking the DD would be set up from the following month. 'Well Dolly' she said, 'I'll be able to buy enough food for you until pension day, but I don't think there'll be much left for me.'

She came out of the Supermarket with four tins of dog food and a packet of dog biscuits. She also had a small loaf, a tin of soup and some margarine. She had just seven pence left. 'There Dolly' she said gently 'at least you'll be alright my darling.'

It was cold now; the weather had turned, and snow was forecast. Mary Lamb sat in her freezing house bundled in cardigans and coats by a one bar electric fire. She'd eaten the soup yesterday and now she toasted a slice of bread on a fork. She was pitifully thin and hunger pangs conspired with the cold to prevent her getting a good night's sleep. Dolly did her best, sleeping on her bed to help keep her warm. 'I might not last this winter through Dolly my darling' she said, 'but my funeral plan is in place and you'll be looked after by those nice people at the charity.'

Mary's daughter Mabel lived over two hundred miles away from her mother. Like many a middle-aged mum, she was kept ultra-busy by the demands of her husband, their three teenage children and a full-time job. She tried to ring her mother once a week, but sometimes that slipped.

Mabel's mum always sounded cheerful on the phone, saying she was saving up to come and see them. She used winter travel as an excuse to put off coming last time they spoke, never admitting she couldn't afford the fare.

Mabel rang Mary and got no reply. Probably nipped out to the shops she told herself and went about cooking the evening meal. At eight thirty she rang again and still got no reply. Now she was worried and rang Mrs Johnstone, her mother's neighbour. She went around and banged on the door but got no response. The Police were called. They broke in and found Mary in bed. She was unconscious and freezing cold, dehydrated and near to death. They rushed her to hospital and Mabel drove up immediately.

They told Mabel it was touch and go. She sat by her bedside all night, stroking Mary's hand, praying. In the morning Mary looked a little better and ate a soft-boiled egg and some toast followed by two cups of tea.

Mabel went to her mother's house and made up

the bed in the spare room. She intended staying until her mother was fully recovered and to look after Dolly. She was surprised at the amount of junk mail her mother received, most of it was from charities seeking donations. But why so many? Mabel thought I don't get a tenth of these.

Suspicion hardened after Mabel had answered several calls from various charities. She told the callers, that her mother was in the hospital. One caller was a persistent, persuasive fellow called Jonas Flint. Mabel worked in sales and recognised his pressure techniques when he tried to get a donation from her. The guy simply wouldn't give up, in the end, she put the phone down on him.

With her mother's reluctant permission, she accessed her bank account. Mabel was shocked by what she found. Three hundred and eighty pounds a month was going out to various charities. No wonder she couldn't afford to eat or heat her house properly. She cancelled all the charity Direct Debits immediately, just before her mum's pension was due to be paid in. Next, she bought her mum a simple pay-as-you-go phone.

Returning to her mother's home, Mabel was just about to ring and have the landline disconnected when the hospital rang, her mother had had a stroke.

Mabel rushed back and was devastated to be told Mary had passed away.

The next day her mother's phone rang again;

Mabel recognised the man's voice, 'ah, Mr Flint' she said, 'I'm glad you've called, I want to inform you that my mother passed away from a stroke yesterday, brought about by acute stress. You, and others of your ilk being largely responsible for that stress. I've cancelled all further payments, there'll be no point in you calling again.'

'Call me Jonas, love' he chirped, relentlessly launching into his sales pitch, 'sorry to hear about your mum and all that. Now, have you considered a donation yourself in your Mum's memory?'

Mabel could hardly believe her ears, his pushiness and crass lack of sensitivity beggared belief. 'Yes, Mr Flint, I have' she said icily, a quiet but intense anger fulminating in her breast 'and the answer is no.' She went on to tell him of her disgust at how her elderly mother had been driven to distraction by charity cold callers.

'Just doing my job, love.' he answered coldly 'just doing my job.'

'No, you're doing much more than that, Mr Flint. I'm a sales manager and I listened to your spiel very carefully last time. You used every manipulator's trick in the book. You are a callous individual and you don't care what misery you cause as long as you achieve your ends.'

'Just doing my job, love' he repeated 'and before you go on preaching, everything I do is legal, see?'

'Tell me, love' Mabel spat, unable now to

contain her anger, 'do you sleep well at night?

'Yeah, I do as it happens' he responded defiantly.

'Well my friend, you won't sleep so peacefully tonight. You see, I inherited certain gifts from my father. You'll be having a cold call yourself soon. A very cold call indeed' she said ominously.

'Yeah, right love, you have me trembling here' his tone turned nasty and sarcastic 'what's the matter, love? Did mummy give away all her lovely money instead of leaving it to you?' Mabel put the phone down.

Next day, the shocked colleagues of Jonas Flint learned that he had suffered a stroke during the night. Later, they heard the prognosis for his future. His mobility and mental capacity would be severely impaired. He'd live like an elderly person for the rest of his days.

Leaving for Good

He punched her splitting her lip as he snatched her purse, sending her reeling backwards. 'Piss off bitch I need that money.' he spat.

'But how will we eat if it's spent on drugs, John?'

His eyes bulged with that out of control rage Mandy knew so well 'use the food bank like the other tossers do' he shouted before turning and slamming the door.

Sarah came creeping downstairs clutching her Teddy, her eyes large and fearful. Seeing the blood on her mother's lip she squeezed the bear tighter to her chest 'are you all right mummy?' Her voice quavered 'can I mend you?'

'Sarah darling, you're only five and mummy is a big girl she can mend herself.'

'Why does he hit you, Mummy?'

'Cos he takes drugs Sarah he's sick sweetheart, that's all.'

'I don't like it when he hits you, Mummy, I'm scared.'

Mandy sat down on the settee and gathered her daughter to her breast ignoring the blood seeping down her chin. She cuddled her, 'there, there, baby don't you worry Mummy will look after you.' They had both been devastated when Sarah's father had left them for another woman then, a year later, she'd met John. At first, things were fine, they both worked hard, and Sarah seemed to settle down; but then he got into drugs.

'Why do people take drugs mummy if it makes them sick?'

Mandy reached for a tissue and dabbed her mouth 'I don't know sweetheart, I wish I did.'

'Will he leave us and go to another lady like daddy did?'

Oh, if only Mandy thought, she was sick of living with John, and Sarah was beginning to be affected by his violence, too. The child seemed reluctant to be in the same room as him and she'd started wetting her bed.

'Will he Mummy? Will he?' Sarah persisted, sounding desperate.

'I don't know baby, why don't you ask him when he's better?'

Sarah flinched, her eyes widened with terror. 'No mummy, no, he'll punish me again.'

Mandy's heart contracted, gripped by a terrible fear 'punish you? What did he punish you for, baby? What has he done you? '

'I can't tell you, mummy, it's secret.'

Mandy's soul froze 'Sarah, darling, has he

touched you anywhere?'

Sarah's eyes welled, and she burst into uncontrollable sobs clutching Mandy around the neck 'he says if I tell he'll hit you and hit you until you die then some people will come and take me away' Sarah wailed 'please mummy, please, if he doesn't hurt you it's alright.'

Mandy's heart almost burst as she rocked Sarah in her bosom, tears streaming down her face; the bastard, she thought, the evil, unspeakable bastard.

Mandy eventually calmed Sarah down and put her to bed. She thought hard. If she reported him now Sarah would be taken into care immediately with all the attendant trauma. No, she would not have that. She sat weighing her options, she had to protect Sarah at all costs, but how? Her fears hardened into a cold hatred. She could knife him as he slept or poison him but that would result in her and Sarah being split up. Sarah had suffered enough. This had to be done right.

Slowly, an idea formed in her mind. Mandy reached into her bra and recovered her meagre reserve. Slipping out of the house to the local off-licence, she bought a bottle of cheap rum and hurried back.

An hour later John returned full of contrition now he'd had his fix. 'Mandy, I'm sorry I hit you, darling, really I am, it won't happen again love honest. Please, forgive me.'

Mandy wanted to scream and shout at him, to thrust a knife into his chest, but she knew this had to be done right. With a supreme effort, she forced a smile and shrugged 'ah well, John, shit happens, here, have a drink, peace offering.'

Soon John was snoring heavily, the empty bottle beside him on the floor where he had collapsed. Mandy went through his pockets finding his remaining drug supply. Having watched him preparing his fix on a few occasions, she knew what to do. Feeling icy calm, she put a ligature around his arm then inserted the needle into his vein. She sat astride him now and slapped him awake. 'I thought I'd tell you before you die, you bastard, I know what you did to my baby Sarah.'

Terror shone in his bulging eyes 'I'm sorry Mandy, honest, I won't touch her again, I swear. I'll leave and never come back. Please.'

'Correct arsehole' she sneered 'you won't be coming back.' Pushing the plunger, she told him 'you're leaving for good.'

Mandy rang the emergency services in the early hours. John's death was registered as simply another tragic O D. Sarah would get her treatment now, it would be a long hard road, but they'd stay together.

No Man's Land

Christmas Eve 1914 the shelling slowed towards nightfall and by 10 p.m. it has ceased entirely. The quietness was almost unbearable. Standing in the trench ankle deep in thick gooey mud Private Albert Bowdell, a fresh-faced nineteen-year-old, listened hard but all he could hear was his own heartbeat. Christmas day would be a good time for the Germans to launch a surprise attack he thought god I hope they don't. He cupped his hands around his cigarette and drew in the comforting smoke. He was deep in the trench so there was no chance of a sniper seeing him. He exhaled slowly listening to the sound of his own breath on the frozen air.

Faintly at first but gradually growing stronger he heard singing, disembodied voices floating in the ether. He looked down the trench but could see no one except the next sentry ten yards away drawing on his pipe. The voices grew louder, and he cocked his ear straining to hear. The words were strange, but the tune was instantly recognisable 'Stille nacht heilige nacht.' Bloody 'ell he thought it's the Hun singing Silent Night. A strongly accented voice carried on the breeze 'Merry Christmas Tommy.'

He felt his spirits lift for the first time in days 'Merry Christmas Fritz' he roared back.

The canvass flap of the dugout lifted, and Captain Rupert Fitzwilliam Charles Bingley-Fortescue emerged looking grim. 'What the hell's going on here Bowdell'? he demanded sternly.

'Oh, Jerry is singing carols and wishing us merry Christmas, sir'

'And did I hear you shouting back, Bowdell?'

'Yes sir' Albert straightened himself up to the attention position.

'Well don't, d'you hear me?' That could be construed as fraternising with the enemy, court-martial, even shot at dawn, you understand?'

Albert suddenly felt depressed again 'Yes sir, sorry sir, won't happen again sir.' He knew from long experience what obsequious words of contrition Bingley-Fortescue wanted to hear.

The captain cycd the private with disdain. The lad was a damn good batman and always kept his kit in tip-top order but, he thought, this man doesn't know his place. The other men were easy to handle but Bowdell, the son of his father's head gamekeeper, had won a scholarship to the grammar school and by all accounts had done rather well. He lived on the estate in the tied cottage with his parents but, breaking with tradition, he didn't work for the family. Instead, his keen intelligence, hard work and diligence, had secured him a junior post in the local bank.

Albert Bowdell had a way of showing an uncommon initiative that disturbed the captain. He'd overheard him in a nearby village speaking very good French to a pretty girl, sourcing extra rations and asking for a date. He suspected this common soldier's knowledge of the language was better than his own. He didn't like that; he didn't like the man's intelligence, his air of independence or the way his fellows looked upon him as a natural leader.

In Bingley-Fortescue's aristocratic view men of the lower social orders, as he thought of them, were there to obey his orders instantly and without question, nothing short of grovelling subservience suited the captain. When addressing his brother officers, he was all charm and politeness, ever the gentleman but, when dealing with his men, he was a cold martinet who would punish a man at the drop of a hat.

After one kit inspection back in England, a comrade had remarked to Albert that the captain had looked down his nose at his immaculate kit laid out on the soldier's bed 'like he'd just been presented with a freshly laid turd' was the soldier's way of expressing it. Finding no fault with the man's kit he had flicked several items off his bed with his swagger stick and simply said 'Not good enough do it again' and walked on to his next victim.

Another reason the captain felt uneasy in the presence of his batman was that he had shot the lad's father. Bowdell senior, as head gamekeeper, had been overseeing the beaters on a pheasant shoot driving the birds onto the guns. The beaters were quite close when the safety whistles blew to stop the shoot. Rupert had been aiming at a bird at that very moment. The bird had unexpectedly dived low and Rupert, who should have held fire, let fly hitting Bowdell senior in the left arm.

Bingley-Fortescue had been feeling rather anxious and out of sorts all that morning and his usual excellent tally of birds was well down largely due to the huge amount of champagne he'd drunk the night before. To make matters worse he'd bet that bragging swine Ellicott fifty guineas he'd do better than him. That now looked like a very forlorn hope. It wasn't the money that bothered him, that wasn't even a consideration; it was the fact that Ellicott would be crowing about it for weeks damn his eyes and now this bloody fellow had gotten himself in front of his gun at the wrong time damn him. The day, he thought, was completely buggered. He felt not the slightest remorse for having shot the man, but he put on a concerned face and made contrite noises in front of his peers. One had to keep up appearances.

'We'll say no more about it this time Bowdell just make sure my Sam Browne is gleaming tomorrow and my pistol is clean I'm off to HQ early.'

'Yes, sir. Goodnight Sir.' Half an hour after his dressing down Albert was relieved of his sentry duty and made his way to the dugout where he would start work cleaning his officer's kit long into the night by the pallid light of a single oil lamp.

Albert had been brought up on the estate of Bullington House a large country pile set in two thousand prime acres on the Welsh borders. He'd been taught to watch his P's and Q's in front of the gentry, always to be polite and compliant with their every wish. As a boy, he had had contact with the young Master Rupert on several occasions mostly during school holidays and had not enjoyed any of them. Rupert boarded at one of the better public schools, so Albert only saw him in the holidays.

One day Rupert had approached him and asked if they taught boxing at his school. Albert said no only football and rugby. Rupert had then told Albert he was going to teach him how to box. Albert knew better than to refuse this son of his father's employer and accepted. On this pretext Rupert, who was three years older than Albert and of a bigger build, had given the younger boy a savage beating eventually walking away smiling saying 'that's the way we deal with clever little shits at my school.'

Albert had learned from a parlour maid that Rupert had suggested to his father that they find a new head gamekeeper and 'throw Bowdell and his useless family out now that the man was a cripple' but Baron Bingley-Fortescue senior, a man of strong moral character, wouldn't hear of it.

It was around ten o'clock on Christmas morning, a cold mist hung in the dank air when a German voice broke the unnatural silence. 'Hey, Tommy, can we come out and bury our sniper you killed last week?' Bill Whatley, Albert's platoon sergeant, suspected a trick at first but peeped through the donkey's ears telescope. There was a German soldier standing on the lip of his trench armed only with a spade. The officers had all gone to a meeting ay HQ i.e. having a Christmas drink behind the lines, so Sergeant Whatley took charge.

'OK' yelled Whatley 'but no tricks or we'll blast you.'

Three more Germans then appeared and moved to the spot about twenty-five yards in front of their lines to where the body of their fallen comrade lay. They dug the grave right there. There was no point taking the decomposing body anywhere else as one piece of mud was very much like another.

After the funeral party had left there was a brief silence then a strong Germanic tenor voice started to sing 'Stille Nacht' again. He was soon joined by other voices and when they had finished the British soldiers, not to be outdone, sang 'Oh Come All Ye Faithful' with great gusto. How the next move came about Albert had no idea but suddenly the German's were out of their trenches and walking across no man's land waving bottles of drink, one of them was even kicking a football. Before Albert could even think about what he was doing, he was following the rest of the men out of the trench to join the throng.

A large German corporal came up to Albert, hand outstretched smiling 'Merry Christmas, have a drink Tommy' he said thrusting a bottle of schnapps into his hand. Albert thanked him and took a long swig.

'My name is Albert what's yours?' he said handing back the bottle.

'I'm Hans, not bloody Fritz!' the man replied with a friendly wink 'And I just knew you wouldn't be called Tommy either'

'No,'

'I'm definitely Albert' he laughed. 'I'm a bank clerk by trade what do you do and how come you speak such good English Hans?'

'I used to represent a company selling toys, we Germans make very good toys you know. I often visited London, indeed my brother has a toy shop there, so I used to visit him quite regularly. He's married to an English lady, been there fifteen years.'

Albert suddenly felt deeply despondent, like a lot of intelligent people he thought a better way of settling differences between nations could and should be found. 'Why the hell are we killing each other, Hans?'

Hans smiled he liked this fresh-faced young Englishman. 'Because we're at war that's all' he said with a philosophical shrug 'countries sometimes go to war and this is one of those sad times.'

Albert, sensing this friendly man was sympathetic to his views, told him of his sadness at the two countries being at war. 'You Germans are Saxons, right?' He didn't wait for an answer but continued in the same breath 'we British are Anglo Saxons, we're cousins for god's sake. Your Kaiser is the grandson of our late Queen Victoria and her husband Albert, after whom I'm named, was a German prince so what the hell is it all about, Hans?' Albert paused for a second but receiving no answer went on 'Why should an ordinary British bank clerk be sent to kill a German farmer in France or a German toymaker be sent to butcher a British bank clerk?' His large expressive brown eyes reflected his sadness and Hans felt for this young man.

'I don't have those answers, Albert, I don't think even the generals do. We are just 'kleine leute' (Little people) you and I, we have no choice but to do as we're told.' He took the proffered cigarette from Albert and sniffed it appreciatively before accepting a light and drawing deeply.

They talked on for some time, sharing Han's schnapps and Albert's fine Virginia cigarettes that Hans liked so much better than his own. At one point they were even drawn briefly into the kick about the others were having. It wasn't a proper game of football as the churned soaked earth would not permit that.

They talked and drank some more, they mixed with the other soldiers but somehow kept coming back and talking to each other showing family photos joking and complaining about their respective officers. These things that all soldiers do but usually confined to their own side.

After a couple of hours, people started drifting back to their own trenches and when the officers returned the stragglers were promptly recalled.

Bingley-Fortescue was not pleased. He was not pleased at all. Severely the worse for the brandy he had consumed he looked balefully at Albert. 'Just last night I warned you about fraternising with the enemy and not twelve hours later I find you doing just that.' The officer's voice was quiet and had a deadly calm quality to it. Albert knew his captain well and recognised this to be a danger sign.

'Sorry sir, I just followed the others, sir.' Albert stood rigidly to attention looking the officer in the eye.

'I didn't warn the others Bowdell, but I did warn you so I'm putting you on a charge of one: wilfully disobeying a lawful command and two: fraternising with the enemy. Do you understand?'

Albert's heart sank. Oh god was he going to be shot by his own side? 'Yes, sir.' Was all he could manage in a wooden voice that betrayed no emotion.

Bingley-Fortescue paused for a moment eyeing

his batman with a mixture of curiosity and a grudging admiration at the lad's calmness. He knew Albert was an intelligent lad and the full implications of what he'd just said would have sunk in immediately. Still, he thought an example needed to be set so the other men knew orders were to be obeyed instantly and without question. Discipline must be maintained and by demonstrating that even the cleverest of them were no match for their superiors it would send out a strong message in a clear way understandable by all.

'Do you realise the full implications of these charges Bowdell?' There was a cruel half gloating note in the officer's voice now. Before Albert could answer Bingley-Fortescue went on 'each charge alone could see you imprisoned for a very long time if not executed, both together will almost certainly put you before a firing squad. Not only that but the disgrace brought on your family will mean they would no longer be employable on my father's estate. Thanks to you your father and mother will be sent away penniless and homeless.'

The captain watched carefully for a reaction but was disappointed when Albert merely replied 'yes sir' in a flat voice that again bore no emotion. 'Am I under arrest sir?'

Bingley-Fortescue eyed Albert Bowdell with something between contempt and pity. He was surprised that Bowdell had not sought to mitigate his behaviour, not pleaded for another chance, not that he would have been given one. The captain replied, a casual almost bored note creeping into his voice 'my kit needs cleaning and I'll consult HQ first as to the best place to send you in the meantime get about your duties. Oh, and send Sergeant Whatley to see me at once.' The captain waved a dismissive hand to indicate he'd finished for the moment.

The generals in their mighty wisdom had decided that this Christmas day meeting with the enemy would be extremely bad for morale back home. In order to keep up the recruitment numbers, the Germans had to be vilified, portrayed as the Hun, evil villains capable of bashing out new born babies brains with their rifle butts not ordinary decent young blokes like their own menfolk. No, courts-martial for these 'offences' were quite out of the question as was any mention in the press. Best it was buried, hushed up for the sake of the war effort.

This decision left Bingley-Fortescue with a large splash of egg on his face. He told Albert in his condescending way that he had reconsidered in the light of the devastation it would cause the soldier's family, them being loyal family servants and all. 'But, should you offend again, I'll shoot you myself Bowdell. Dismiss.'

An uneasy truce settled between the captain and his servant neither of them spoke to the other unless it was strictly necessary. This went on for a week or so until the day of the big push, the New Year offensive. The artillery barrage had started at two o'clock the day before the attack and continued until dawn when it abruptly ceased. Whistles blew, and they went over the top. Albert had to stick close to his captain as he was his runner and would carry messages to other parts of the line as and when told.

One thing no one could accuse Bingley-Fortescue of was cowardice he charged forward like a man possessed, pistol in hand, shouting encouragement to his company at the top of his voice. They had progressed about twenty yards toward the enemy lines when the machine gunners opened fire cutting large swathes through the attackers. Men were falling on either side of Albert but by some miracle, it seemed he and his officer were left unharmed. It went on like this for the next few minutes. The insane stutter of machine guns, men's screams as they were hit and now the German artillery had opened fire the shells making orange splashes of death among them.

'Keep going men we're nearly there' yelled Bingley-Fortescue just a second before a bullet ripped through his thigh right. Albert went to his assistance as a bullet passed through his sleeve without touching him. He dragged the pale-faced officer into a deep shell hole and dived in with him just as a shell exploded nearby, the concussion from it deafening and disorienting him.

'We'll be alright here for the moment sir,' said Albert recovering slightly 'I'll get you patched up as best I can sir.'

'Get me back to our lines Bowdell, I simply have to report that the Hun has twice as many machine guns as we anticipated.' Even hurt as he was the captain still had the ring of authority in his voice. Albert bent down and got an arm under the officer's shoulder. He lifted him with some difficulty then half carried half dragged him up the slope of the shell hole. Immediately his head cleared to top a machine gunner sprayed a burst at them narrowly missing both. Albert dropped his charge and they slid down the muddy side together into the stinking pool of slime below.

'I'm afraid they've got our range, sir,' he said 'we'll have to wait until dark before we move.'

'Hell, man, it's your duty to get me back to our lines, it can't wait all bloody day, HQ simply have to know about those guns. '

Albert looked doubtful 'but sir if we try now, we won't make it at least we'll have a chance in the darkness, sir.'

Bingley-Fortescue saw this sensible argument as gross insubordination, the agony of his wound did nothing for his temper nor rational thought. He slowly raised his pistol and pointed it at Albert then even more slowly he cocked it. 'I told you I'd shoot you myself if you failed to carry out my orders,' he said in a flat hard voice. 'Last chance help me up Bowdell.'

Albert looked down the hexagonal barrel of the big Webley pistol. He stared for a moment in mute defiance 'Well, if you shoot me that's both of us buggered then' he said sullenly omitting the 'sir' in his address, a point not missed by the officer.

The pistol sounded loud in the confines of the shell hole the bullet striking the earth a mere two inches from Albert's head. 'The next one will kill you Bowdell now help me up.' Albert moved slowly towards the stricken man his anger didn't show but he wanted to kill this arrogant bastard. Once again, he picked him up and once more they moved painfully slowly towards the lip of the shell crater. They got a little further this time as the machine gunner waited until they made a bigger target. Just as he thumbed the trigger to release his fatal burst a British bullet glanced off his gun with a loud whine startling him and causing him to jerk as he fired.

The bullets went low but came close splashing around their feet one of them taking off two of Albert's toes. He screamed with pain as they fell back down the slope. Albert felt the slime close over his head the agony from his foot momentarily forgot in his desperation to surface and spit out the choking filth that filled his mouth. Taking great gasps of air Albert, now on his hands and knees, looked around him and saw his captain struggling to turn himself over.

Despite his own pain he crawled to assist the more seriously injured man. He laid him as gently as he could on the slope of the shell hole as far out of the water as he could get him. 'You alright sir?' he asked.

'No bloody thanks to you Bowdell, you incompetent bastard.' Bingley-Fortescue's face was grey and ravaged with pain, there was a savagery in the man's voice now. Usually so controlled in his viciousness he was feeling helpless and frustrated, his leg hurt like hell.

Around them the attack had faltered and those who were able had staggered back to their lines helping what wounded they could. The moans of the other wounded and dying that couldn't be saved were pitiful to hear. One poor soul was repeatedly calling for his mother his cries getting weaker and weaker until they finally stopped after what had seemed like an eternity.

Albert dug in his pocket and produced a battered packet of cigarettes. He lit one and handed it to the captain 'Smoke'? Bingley-Fortescue took the offered cigarette ignoring the insolence of the lack of a 'sir.' Albert lit one for himself and sank back against the mud wall of their prison. He eyed his companion speculatively. 'They'll probably come at last light to either finish us off or take us prisoner' Albert said dully 'Either way if we try to get out of here again, we'll be dead and now I'm wounded too I won't be able to carry you.'

Still refusing to use a respectful 'sir' address Albert watch his captain's reaction and seeing none said peevishly 'If you're thinking of shooting me then bloody well get on with it, you miserable bastard.'

Bingley-Fortescue looked at him with a cold hatred. 'You are an insolent bastard Bowdell and no mistake. Well, let me make it clear to you that if we do get out of this mess, I'll see you court-martialled for insubordination.'

Albert couldn't have cared less at that moment his foot was throbbing, he was seriously thirsty, and he was both physically and emotionally exhausted. His Captain was speaking again. 'I'll make certain your family are thrown off the estate, too, they'll die in penury and all due to you Bowdell, all due to you.' He paused briefly scowling then went on: 'I believe your cousins work for Mr Ellicott? Well, they can kiss their working lives goodbye, too. Off, with no references, no one will employ them, *ever*. He spat out the last word angrily.

Albert dragged himself over to where the wounded officer had ceased his diatribe for the moment and was sucking on his cigarette. He was filled with a cold rage, trembling in his anger and now beyond caring what happened to him. The arrogance of this man who thought he could control him by threatening his family was just too much.

Albert knocked the cigarette out of the captain's

hand and gripped him by the collar. Utter shock and surprise registered on Bingley-Fortescue's face. 'Listen to me you over-privileged prick' he shouted 'I'm tired of your bullying, tired of you treating me as less than dog shit on your boots. Who the fuck do you think you are, eh? So, you live in a big house with servants to wipe your arse, so your daddy has lots of money and you feel so bloody superior to everyone else. Why? What have you ever done? What can you do? You can't even clean your own kit, and you call yourself a soldier? If I could find my rifle, I'd blow your stupid useless bloody head off!'

Albert was spent now he sunk down beside the wounded officer breathing heavily. Both men were silent, the captain stunned at the venom in Albert's voice then, mercifully, it started to rain. They lay with their mouths open to the sky every drop they caught a blessed relief. Hours went by as they drifted in and out of consciousness weakened by shock and blood loss.

After what seemed like hours Bingley-Fortescue began talking to no one in particular. 'I'm superior because of my elevated birth,' he said sounding like he was trying to convince himself. 'My family are aristocracy you see, and we have certain privileges and we have a great responsibility also. We must look after the land and, to some extent, the people who work for us, too. Not that the lower classes understand of course. Not many know their place these days it comes from educating them you know, no good will come of it mark my words.'

Albert heard this rambling speech as if in a dream, he knew the Bingley-Fortescue family history, of course, everyone on the estate knew. He could no longer summon the energy to be angry but said in a tired voice 'the only difference between you and me is money Rupert and that's all. You can afford to buy your privileged position and the likes of me can't. Your family made its money in the slave trade. Your great, great grandfather was a thief who stole people and sold them into slavery and you still buy and sell people today. The only difference is that today you have to pay them a pittance and tie them in a cottage or a pathetic little room in your attic but they're slaves by another name that's all.' There was no accusation or bitterness in Albert's voice it was just a plain statement.

There was silence for a moment then Rupert said 'One cannot expect a person of your breeding to understand Bowdell. You've had a smattering of education and that's your problem, you're educated beyond your intelligence that's all. As for money, that is such a vulgar subject...'

Albert interrupted him abruptly. 'Money? Vulgar? The only people I've ever heard calling money vulgar are those snooty bastards like you who have far more than is good for them' he continued in the same flat monotone 'anyway, your sort will be washed away by this war when people realise just what mindless butchers you and your so-called class are, they'll never be dominated by you again. No matter what happens to us now Rupert the die is cast. You and your sort are finished.'

The light was fading now and the captain, talking to himself as much as to Albert summed up their situation. 'They'll be sending out rescue parties shortly and the German's will come out looking too, so it depends on who reaches us first I suppose. Probably the Germans because they're closest. I believe they are quite civilised towards officers you know so I will be looked after in a half decent fashion. On the other hand, Bowdell, you will be sent to rot in some hell-hole somewhere a long way from home. Either way, I'll survive and you, *dear Albert*, are finished. He used Albert's forename with an exaggerated mock politeness that reinforced his threat to ruin him and his family.

The same cold rage rose again in Albert's breast, how dare this arrogant bastard play god with him? How had the baron, a thoroughly decent man whom Albert had great respect for, managed to breed this hateful creature?

A plan was forming in Albert's mind even as he heard German voices approaching their shell hole. Quickly Albert took up the officer's pistol broke it and checked the load. One bullet left that was all he needed. 'I have some good news for you, Rupert,' he said coldly 'You're going to be a hero, my friend.'

'What the hell are you talking about? Give me that pistol at once man!' There was a note of uncertainty in his voice now, even fear. The guttural voices were drawing ever closer and time was short.

'Well, it's like this Rupert, we were trapped you and I and you, noble person that you are, fought bravely and when you were down to your last bullet you turned the gun on yourself. Death before dishonour and all that shit.'

'You ...You wouldn't dare! Bingley-Fortescue looked aghast at Albert as the seriousness of the young private's intention sunk in. 'It's murder, I'm your superior officer, they'll shoot you, man.'

Albert smiled 'Who'll know? Anyway, I probably won't last the night out, so I'll see you in hell, my *dear* Rupert.' The German voices were mere yards away now as Albert pushed the gun under Rupert's chin and squeezed the trigger.

The shot alerted the searching soldiers to his position and a voice barked an order. Albert stood up as best he could and put his hands in the air. One of the soldiers fired in his direction but it was a wild shot. Albert couldn't have cared less at that moment, his foot was throbbing, he'd lost a lot of blood and he was seriously thirsty. He was both physically and emotionally exhausted. A voice spoke sharply, and the man who'd fired lowered his rifle.

A familiar figure slid down into the hole to stand in front of him smiling. It was Hans. 'Hello Albert,' he said grinning 'for you the war is over you lucky man' Hans bent to check out the officer, removing the field notebook from the dead man's pocket. He noted the powder burns around the bullet hole.

'What happened here?' he asked.

Albert looked into Han's questioning face. 'He wouldn't surrender, and he was down to his last bullet, so he shot himself when he heard you coming.'

'Really?' Hans looked incredulous. 'Did he believe we German's are savages who would not accept an honourable surrender?'

Albert shrugged 'He was an aristocrat, strange people British aristocrats, death before dishonour, that sort of thing.'

Hans nodded, understanding creeping over his face. 'Ah yes, we have officers like that, too, all personal honour and duelling scars.'

Walking through the barbed wire into the German trenches. Albert was sickened to pass within two feet of Sgt Whatley's body suspended in the wire.

It was 1919 before Albert got back home to tell his story of how the gallant captain, though badly wounded, had fought to the last and had died bravely saving his life. The suicide story had been good enough for the Germans but those who knew the

Captain wouldn't have swallowed it. Albert had had plenty of time to get his new story right and mentally rehearsed it to perfection. No hyperbole, no frills, just a tale of exemplary courage simply told. On the strength of this, the late Captain Rupert Fitzwilliam Charles Bingley-Fortescue was posthumously awarded the military cross.

Rupert's father had died whilst they were away fighting, the estate was being run by his widow. Lady Dorothy was a kindly soul and often came to see Albert's parents during their retirement years

Albert eventually married the local vicar's daughter and moved away to become the youngest manager ever to be appointed by his bank. The times were changing.

Cats and Bags

I awoke screaming, consumed by feelings of guilt and horror. I knew I'd killed her. I saw again the silhouette of her body sliding into the hole, heard the soft thud as it hit the grave's bottom.

Sandra switched the light on 'Oh, for god's sake! Really, Frank, I can't take much more of this' she snapped. She sounded more angry than usual.

'If you hadn't let the spare room out whilst I was overseas, I could have slept there.' I said defensively.

'Right then, while you're at your therapist's appointment tomorrow I'll tell her to go, OK?'

I felt a pang of guilt. The woman had done me no harm but now she would be turfed out at short notice. There was not exactly a glut of decent rooms to be had in Oldham.

Why did the old hag next door screech for her damned cat at three a.m. every morning, dragging me from my drug-induced oblivion? All I craved was sleep, to forget the horrors. But no, her sodding cat came first. After five consecutive nights I was at the end of my tether 'I'm just back from Afghanistan' I told her 'I'm finding sleep very difficult, 'please, just buy a cat flap; I'll install it for free' I pleaded.

'Huh' she snorted, scowling at me, her piggy little eyes filled with spite 'I know you, you're that weirdo who sleep-walks. Didn't the police bring you home last week?'

'Yes, yes, I'm having a few problems I admitted, 'now, about your cat......'

'Sod off, weirdo' she screamed in my face.

It was too much for my frazzled nerves 'you stupid old bag' I yelled, 'I've a damned good mind to poison your bloody cat. How would you like that?'

I saw the terror in her eyes as she hurriedly retreated, slamming her door.

Now, everything was a drug haze in my mind. I had taken a double dose of my sleeping pills in the hope of getting a decent night's sleep, but it was not to be. I heard again the machine gun's insane chatter, I felt the blast as a rocket propelled grenade exploding nearby. I saw my mate Charlie rolling around in the smoke and dust screaming, both his legs gone. Then her screeching started, endless screeching for her damned cat! I couldn't separate dreams from reality. I couldn't remember the actual deed, but I knew I'd killed her. The vision of her dark silhouette sliding into that dread hole kept replaying in my mind.

Before dawn I arose and dressed quietly so as not

to disturb Sandra. I went into the garden to confirm what I already knew. There, under the apple tree, was the freshly covered grave. I went to the garage where I kept a tow rope. I couldn't face endless years in prison.

At six, I went into Alexandra Park; there would be a suitable tree there I could use. I wandered past the magnificent Victorian pavilion, the dawn mist looked beautiful drifting in wraiths across the still boating lake. I walked on in a daze until I came to the of the statue of Joseph Howarth.

We'd learned about Joe at school, he was a remarkable man. Born blind in 1786, he was Oldham's Town Crier for forty years. A man with a razor-sharp memory, he was also a preacher and could recite the bible chapter and verse. He ran had a pie stall on Tommyfield market as well.

Now, as I looked up at him, his walking stick in his right hand and his Town Crier's bell in his left, I recalled that Mrs Gailbraith taught us that whenever we felt our problems were too great, just remember what Joe achieved in spite of blindness. He could have lived the life of a beggar like so many with his affliction did in those days. But Joe took responsibility for his life, letting nothing stop him. And Alexandra park itself had been created by redundant mill workers thrown onto the scrap heap by the cotton famine caused by the American Civil war. They hadn't given up on life. They, like blind

Joe, had taken responsibility for their future.

A blackbird began his lovely song in the nearby tree that I'd chosen to end my life on, defying me to use his haven for so dark a purpose. As I watched the sunrise, my senses slowly started to return from my drug-induced muddle. The sun slanted its light across this place of beauty created from hope.

I sat down on the statue's plinth regarding the rope in my hand. Joe must have been tempted to end it all sometimes. A lot of the Mill workers, too.

You're a soldier Frank I told myself. Why the coward's way out? You're a corporal, a leader of men. Stop whining and start shining. Take responsibility for what you've done.

At eight, I walked into Oldham police station. 'I murdered my neighbour last night' I told them.

Detectives questioned me with a lawyer present. I confessed, telling them all I could remember.

'And you reckon you were sleep walking at the time?'

'I must have been, everything's so vague but her grave is there as proof.'

'OK sir, we'll pop you into a cell whilst further enquiries are made.'

Many hours passed before they came for me.

'Right, Mr Williams, we're releasing you into the custody of a psychiatric hospital sir, your condition is far more serious than was first diagnosed.'

'What about the murder?' I asked.

'You didn't kill anyone, sir' he said, looking at me like I was an object of pity. 'Let me explain. At three thirty this morning your neighbour, Mrs Paisley, rang the police to say that you and your wife had killed her cat and were burying it in your garden' he looked embarrassed 'we get a lot of these calls; we arranged a PCSO visit for later today.'

'So, what's happened? I asked.

'We searched your garden, sir, where we recovered the body of one Miss Jane Phillips, your lodger and, whilst you were overseas, your wife's lover.'

I knew Sandra had occasionally slept with women before we met but she said that it had been purely experimental.

'Miss Phillips resented being demoted from lover to lodger and threatened to reveal all to you. Your wife was tiring of you both and saw a way of killing two birds with one stone so to speak. She knew your mental state was very fragile, that you'd mentioned suicide before. She slipped Miss Phillips some of your sleeping medicine then garrotted her with your army boot laces, burying them with her. During the burial, you sleep-walked onto the scene. Your wife guided you back to bed and gave you more sleeping drugs.

'And Sandra has confessed? Why?'

'She didn't have much choice, sir, Mrs Paisley witnessed her digging and you standing watching.

The hedge was in the way, so she couldn't see what was being buried and assumed, in light of your earlier threat, that it was her missing cat.'

Zen on Zen

Amanda descended to the side of the great Ro-Ro ferry following Robert. She pinched her nostrils closed through her mask and blew, feeling her ears pop. He landed on the ship's side, turned and gave her the OK sign before immediately plunging off, doing a rapid descent forty metres down to the wreck's propellers. Show-off she thought, there was no way she would follow him at that speed. She felt a nervous shudder down her spine. Surely, he wouldn't try to kill her on this dive, it was just her over-active imagination she decided.

They'd dived the day before and all seemed fine but last night and this morning he'd been unusually quiet. She knew he was jealous of her wealth, his snide remarks after he'd been drinking made that clear enough.

Last night she had tried to seduce him, but he couldn't manage it.

'Amanda my love, we're diving the Zenobia early tomorrow and I'm a little anxious, that's all. Sorry.'

Amanda's mouth turned down at the corners, her eyes narrowed, and a frown creased her brow, 'but you've dived the Zenobia dozens of times, Robert, surely you can't be that nervous?'

'I'm not nervous for me Amanda, I'm nervous for you. You've only just qualified as an advanced open water diver, and you've been down to forty metres so few times.' His dark brown eyes looked serious. The lines etched deeply on his suntanned face giving him an almost haggard look 'I do worry about you. You place far too much faith in that stupid Zen meditation stuff you're into.' He scowled, wagging a cautionary finger 'trying to keep calm by thinking OM at forty metres when things go wrong is just not possible.'

Amanda smiled, you silly boy, I've dived to forty-two metres in Wastwater and in Dorothea quarry, too. If I can dive those deep dark dangerous places, then the warm Med with its excellent a visibility shouldn't phase me. And, my darling, I'll have you with me. My very own Open Water Scuba Instructor with dozens of dives on the Zen.'

He frowned at her 'You can't call it the Zen until you've dived it' he said peevishly.

She frowned right back, 'don't be childish Robert and, by the way, Zen meditation isn't stupid, you should try it yourself, you'd sleep a lot better.'

He went to protest but she held up her hand, looking forlornly at his flaccid manhood 'enough, let's go to the bar, I feel like a drink or is that verboten too?'

Amanda looked obliquely at him as he ordered their drinks, assessing the tenseness in him. She knew men. Oh, boy, did she know men. Something was wrong. Her instinct for these things was something she trusted. She had paid for this holiday because he was having cash flow problems he said. 'I'm a bit extended at the moment darling' he'd told her, it's due to paying large deposits on two London flats plus I've had some hefty repair bills to fork out for, too.'

She knew that was a lie he'd been gambling with those Russian so-called friends of his again.

Now, as she sank ever deeper, she wondered had he ever really loved her? Was it all about her money? She hoped she was wrong, but Robert did talk in his sleep even if indistinctly. The name Sophie was repeated several times so was "her money." Amanda knew Sophie was a pole dancer whom he'd slept with him before they met.

People assumed Amanda had been born into great wealth simply because the new surname she'd chosen was Getty, her mother's maiden name. She was in no way related to the famous Getty family and never claimed to be. It didn't do her any harm, though, to let people assume that she was related whilst she maintained an air of mysterious silence. She had been born on a Wythenshawe council estate in Manchester, her father a bricklayer and her mother a chef. She'd left home at the age of eighteen to become a high-class escort worker before running her own chain of successful massage parlours. This was her secret known to very few up North and none in London. Her profits had been invested in property just before the boom. At the age of thirty-four, she'd sold up and moved to London where she re-invested her money shrewdly in property. London prices soared and her fortunes with it. A few elocution lessons whilst acquiring a knowledge of art and fine wine and she had re-invented herself, not that anyone gave a damn anyway.

Then she'd met Robert, a tough cockney commodities trader, at a presentation for property investors. He had impressed her with his good looks, self-confidence and boyish charm. Their marriage came after only six weeks of heady parties and wild sex. He had the body of a Greek god and was into scuba diving. She'd learned to dive to please him and then found she loved it.

They'd had the dive boat to themselves. Mid-week towards the end of the season was always quiet so when Robert said he wanted to hire the whole boat and offered well above the odds, the dive operator had quickly agreed. That morning there was only one other boat about, it was anchored at the wreck's bow.

She followed Robert through the huge propellers to the seabed. After ten minutes exploring the old trucks that had been on the great Ro-Ro Robert checked his computer and started a gradual ascent towards the bridge, In the distance, two other divers in rebreathers glided silently in their bubble-free gear.

Robert suddenly turned to her and gave the follow me signal. She thought they had been going to explore the bridge, but Robert swam through a hatch into the interior. She switched her torch on. As she swam after him a great Moray eel came out of the hatch. She was awestruck as the huge creature glided past her its movements so fluid and graceful that it seemed to be made of the ocean itself. Then Robert turned and signalled again impatiently. She checked her air, 120 bar, roughly half of her fifteen litre tank. She'd be OK to make the bow as long as they progressed gradually upwards. This was not the dive they had planned, she'd never done a wreck penetration course, but she was with him, so all should be well. A chill struck her momentarily, had she been right? Was there something amiss? She told herself not to be silly. Murder? He was her loving husband for God's sake.

Robert slowly led her down a narrow corridor to a door in what was now the floor. He lifted it with some difficulty and pointed into it like there was something of great interest in there.

She swam closer and shone her torch into the yawning gap. Nothing! It was only a small empty storeroom. That was when she flipped onto her back and saw him with his hand outstretched, a murderous gleam in his torch-lit eye. He was going to turn her air off. He looked surprised for a second then continued to close on her. He tore the regulator out of her mouth and hugged her to him, reaching around her for her air valve.

A feeling of desperation engulfed her. She grabbed his mask tearing it off his face and letting it fall behind her. He let her go and started thrashing about desperate to retrieve the mask. Without it he was blind.

Amanda kicked out, her large fins slowing her action, but she succeeded in placing her right foot against him pushing herself away far enough to grab her spare regulator from around her neck and stuff it into her mouth. She urgently drew in great gulps of air as her heart raced. It wasn't over yet.

Though blind for all practical purposes and the sea water stinging his eyes, Robert could still see her torchlight and finned quickly towards it, clawing wildly at her, kicking up clouds of silt until the water around them resembled milky tea. She twisted away as his hand closed on her arm. She felt wild panic start to grip her. No, it couldn't end like this she had too much to live for.

She reached for his regulator and using both hands managed to drag it out of his mouth. He was forced to let her go and grab his spare giving her precious seconds to swim away. She had to clear her head, she had to think. She switched her torch off. Darkness would hide her.

As she swam away, she resisted the urge to fin like crazy although she did change from the frog kicking action they'd used to prevent silt from being disturbed and started the normal up and down stroke. This was quicker and would kick up the silt making Roberts chances of catching her even slimmer.

She thudded into the wall in the darkness banging her head then started feeling her way along it. behind her she could see his torch as Robert, too, followed the wall; she must not allow him to catch her.

Air was now her concern, she's been breathing hard and raggedly during the struggle and fear increased with the darkness, her heart was pounding, her breathing rate far too rapid. She'd never find her way out and to the surface at this rate. She started her Zen meditation chant in her head, deliberately slowing her breathing. She felt her heart rate begin to slow as she became aware of her body from head to toe.

Robert was now desperate. He flashed his torch left and right looking for her though he could only see but a few blurred inches. Vanity had prevented him packing a spare mask, he had not wanted its bulk spoiling the manly leg line of his wetsuit. He finned powerfully now, he had to catch her before the end of the corridor.

Amanda glanced behind her. His torch was

closing fast. What should she do? She dumped some air from her jacket and allowed herself to sink to the floor. She lay still as he passed over her. Surely her bubbles would give her away. They did.

Robert felt rather than saw her bubbles hit him in the face. He reached down and grabbed her shoulder. She did her best to fight him off, but he had the strength of a demon. He felt for her mask. If he could take it off her, she'd be blind and he would be able to see. She would be at his mercy. With her right hand she held on to it, with her left she dug her thumbnail deep into his eye. He recoiled then came towards her again, this time he grabbed at her regulator. She realised then that there were no bubbles coming from his. He was out of air. She kicked and struggled and at last, she was free. Above her she saw Roberts struggles weaken, his torch fell away and hung by its lanyard, the useless regulator slipped from his mouth, then Robert was still.

Amanda made her way more slowly now with measured strokes and breathing, the Zen chant in her head keeping her calm. She resisted the urge to check her air, it didn't matter now, she'd either live or die. Knowing she was about to run out would only cause her to panic and use even more. She continued along the seemingly endless corridor, breathing slowly, calmly her heart rate now almost normal. At last, she came to an open space. She was still inside the ship but there was light above. She ascended now and glanced at her computer, she was at twenty-three metres with twelve bar of air left. She'd need to resist the urge to dash for the surface. Keeping a careful eye on her computer, she began her ascent, the device told her she needed a five-minute decompression stop at five metres. No chance of that so she'd need to visit a decompression chamber. It could be worse.

As her head broke the surface her air ran out, there was none to inflate her buoyancy jacket. Now her problem was to stay on the surface as she bobbed in the gentle swell, her mouth at the level of the water. She reached down with both hands and found the toggles and pulled. Her lead weights fell away, and she rose in the water. Then she heard the engine as the boatman had realised something was wrong and came to pick her up. She had survived thanks to her use of Zen on the Zen

The Author and the Nutter

A chance meeting on a bus that gave everyone a laugh (Except the author)

As the bus ground its way slowly through the rush hour traffic I sat nursing my dark thoughts. Would I ever get my bloody novel finished? I'd had people on my back for a month now wanting this changed or that chapter re-written. I couldn't even see through the sodding windows, they were all steamed up. My damp, clammy shirt was clinging to me like a whore on payday, making me shiver.

Greater Manchester Transport had done its worst yet again. Forty minutes I had waited at the shelterless bus stop in the rain, not a taxi to be had. Then, of course, two buses turned up at once. I boarded wearily. I needed a stiff drink, a hot bath and my bed.

At the next stop I heard him get on, Nigel the nutter, his over-loud, over-enthusiastic voice regaling the poor sodden sods boarding with him.

Oh, Christ, I prayed, please don't let him sit next to me, please.

Of course, the bugger made a bee-line for me.

'Hi' he chirped, proffering a pudgy hand 'I'm Nigel.'

I ignored the hand and simply nodded at him. Oh shit, I thought in despair. I had nothing to read and my phone was charging at home. Should I feign sleep? No, I might miss my stop.

'What do you do? Nigel quipped brightly.

'Not a lot.'

'What does not a lot consist of?' he boomed, his eager bonhomie grating on my nerves.

I squirmed, I really didn't need this. 'I do a bit of writing' I mumbled, hoping that would immediately bore him. It does with most people.

'Oh wow, he exclaimed what sort of stuff do you write?

I very nearly said knitting patterns in the hope of closing him down, but the nutty git would probably turn out be demon knitter.

'Fiction.'

What, adventure stuff, murder, war and the like?' His moon face was the colour and texture of cold porridge from which his tiny bright blue eyes twinkled like fairy lights.

'I read a lot of Andy McNab' he said without waiting for an answer 'and his mate that Chris what's-his-name, but both those guys are obviously big bullshitters.'

My eyebrows arched into my hairline in total disbelief 'Do you mean Chris Ryan?'

'Oh yes, Ryan, that's the one' Nigel said blithely, twisting towards me 'no bloke could ever survive all the shit situations they put their hero's through.'

'It's fiction' I said in exasperation 'escapism, that's all.'

'Well they should write only the truth' Nigel said petulantly, his mouth losing its annoying grin for a moment.

'Then it wouldn't be fiction' I said 'it would be history, a bit mundane and boring.'

'But if they really were in the SAS, they must have lots of real stories to write about.'

He was really beginning to boil my piss now. I can tolerate your average nutter, enjoy them even, but Nigel was in a class if his own. I remained silent. The woman sitting behind me giggled at my discomfiture, she was really enjoying the show.

I turned. She was young, black with an intelligcnt face and dressed as garishly as Donald Trump's Christmas tree. I glared at her curling my lip and she suddenly found her phone of overwhelming interest.

'I fired a real gun once you know' Nigel piped up, abruptly changing the subject 'have you ever fired one?'

'I used to be a soldier.'

'For real?' Naw!'

Jesus, I thought, this guy's an expert at getting up my nose. He sits beside me, imposes a conversation on me that I don't bloody well want and then starts slagging off two of my favourite authors.

'Yes mate, for real'

'Were you an SAS man then?'

'No, Artillery.'

'Oow, long range snipers, eh? Miles behind the front line. They call you the 'drop shorts', don't they?' he said with an inane grin.

I wanted to strangle the sod there and then. Was he really so thick he couldn't see how insulting he was being? His grin grew wider, expecting me to laugh. Yup, he was a full-blown nutter alright.

I glared at him 'there was no front line in Northern Ireland, Nigel, we all did the same job.'

'Oh sorry' he quipped and nudged me in the ribs, his stupid grin getting wider 'I was only joking.' He abruptly changed the subject back to writing. 'What's your name? Are you someone I've heard of or just some unpublished wanna-be amateur?'

I groaned inwardly, *God give me strength*. I wanted to scream 'look, pal, why don't you just piss off and find another seat?' But, of course, I'm a normal polite person and my stop was just a couple more away. I bit my tongue. Patience, I told myself, nothing lasts forever.

'Well….?'

'I'm not telling you my name' I said, not quite succeeding in keeping my irritation from showing 'I use a pseudonym.'

'Why not? Don't you like me? You don't, do

you?' His fat lips trembled, and he looked like a hurt kid.

'It's not that.'

'Well, what name do you write under then?' he persisted 'Are you someone famous?' his voice boomed around the lower deck, people were grinning from ear to ear at the unexpected entertainment.

At long last I reached my stop, got up and squeezed past him. As I did so an evil idea flashed into my mind. I turned and leaned down into the nutter's face giving him as mean a look as I could muster 'I write, Nigel, under the name of McNab, Andy McNab.'

He looked at me in utter terror, shrinking away, his pudgy frame tight against the window, his pudding face ashen. For the first time since he climbed aboard the bus, the bugger was silent. 'Bye now' I growled 'mind how you go.' I made my way off the bus with a feeling of wild, unholy joy in my heart.

The bloke who'd got off behind me tapped me on the shoulder. I turned to see this squat, hard-looking bugger with piercing eyes.

'I understand why you did that mate, he said, 'but don't take my name in vain again, OK?'

The Colour of Courage

She had barely opened the pub when the two half-drunk American airmen came in. The Lieutenants from Burtonwood air base swaggered across to a table by the window. 'Hey, let's have a couple of beers over here' the one wearing the expensive leather jacket and dark sunglasses yelled.

Margot hated arrogance, 'drinks are served at the bar, sir.'

'That so?' Lieutenant Jackson Cleveland said peering over his rims 'well, I'm used to better service from bar girls. Who's in charge around here anyway?'

Margot's widower father, Brian Greenwood, entered from behind the bar curtain 'that would be me sir.' He started drawing beer. The lieutenants sat down placing their feet on the table in an act of calculated provocation. Brian saw Margot bristle and quickly intervened 'would you fetch some beer mats please, Margot?' She shrugged angrily and left with a defiant toss of her head.

Brian carried the beers over 'your drinks, gentlemen.'

Cleveland threw a coin onto the table 'keep the change barman.'

Brian refused the bait 'thank you, sir.'

Margot returned with the mats in time to see the black captain enter the bar. He walked up to her smiling, his large athletic frame moving gracefully. Margot's knees went weak. He was beautiful.

'Excuse me ma'am' he drawled 'do you have lemonade please?'

Lt. William Pickmore, Cleveland's companion, slammed his beer down. 'Where I come from, we don't serve coloureds in the same bars as whites.'

It was a provocation too far. 'Well, you're not where you come from now, mister. Over here we serve everyone' Margot glared defiantly 'if you don't like it, leave.'

Cleveland looked at Brian 'You let the hired help shoot their mouths off like that?'

'The hired help is my daughter mister and I agree with her.' Brian walked over to the table and lifted their drinks. 'I served in the trenches alongside Indians, Africans and Ghurkhas and the blood I saw spilt was all the same colour. Time you left, gentlemen.'

As he turned back to the bar Cleveland leapt up and grabbed his shoulder raising his fist.

'You strike that man, you'll leave here on a stretcher.' the black captain barked 'In case it passed your notice Lieutenant, I'm your superior officer.'

'I don't take orders off'n a negro.'

The captain stepped between Brian and the pair, shoulders squared, 'Captain Silas T Jazzbohne at your service.'

Cleveland held Pickmore back. 'You the Jazzbohne that won the Golden Gloves back in 1940?'

'The same lieutenant, now, unless there's something else, I suggest you move out.'

The pair sullenly complied, and Silas apologized to Brian and Margot. 'Some of those Southern rich boys still think they're slave owners.' Silas smiled, instantly dispelling the sombre mood 'I came here looking for help, ma'am. My father's a preacher back in Louisiana, in the last war he was a merchant seaman. When he docked in Liverpool, he loved visiting old churches. He asked me to take some photographs.'

Margot smiled 'Any particular churches?'

'One church he really liked was St. Elphin's someplace around here. He reckons there's been a church there since the year 650, that right?'

Margot grinned, local history was her hobby. 'True, Captain, it's the parish church of Warrington. The present church, though, was only opened in 1867.'

'Please, call me Silas.'

'I'm Margot, Miss Margot Greenwood.'

Over the next three months, Margot showed Silas

around on his off-duty days. Using his jeep they visited every old church from Liverpool to Leigh. Inevitably they grew closer until one evening the friendly good night peck became a lingering kiss. They became lovers that night.

*****

Silas eased the B17 bomber around in a wide turn. 'OK, running in, camera ready?' He was part of an experimental team. The top-secret camera in the bomb bay was undergoing final tests.

'Black Belle, Black Belle, we're under attack, divert to Ringway immediately, over.' Silas knew he should obey the tower but just then he saw the enemy bombers three miles away and ten thousand feet below him. He swooped down as they turned for home. Two planes went down immediately; the rest held formation, concentrating their fire on him.

Silas felt the massive jolt as cannon fire ripped away the front gun blister. The sudden, increased drag made the nose drop alarmingly. He took evasive action as his gunners fought back. Another burst of cannon fire tore along the fuselage. His co-pilot, George Benton, died instantly as shrapnel slashed into Silas's legs. Screams came from the 'plane's interior as men were hit.

He dived as another burst of fire ripped along his wings. The starboard outer and port inner engines went on fire. The fire extinguishers were activated, and the flames died, leaving oily smoke trailing.

Silas looked down at his legs. Blood was pooling crimson at his feet. He hit the intercom. 'Bale out, bale out.' The rear gunner managed to jump but the rest were either dead or wounded.

At six thousand feet he managed to gain more control of the stricken plane. His wings were torn to ribbons and the plane juddered violently with every move of the controls.

He called the tower. It would have to be a dangerous down-wind landing; he couldn't risk circling. Silas aimed for the grass alongside the cratered runway. He felt faint now and his vision started to blur.

Silas was feeling weak but incredibly calm. He thought of Margot, his beautiful Margot and a tear ran down his cheek. He could see many of the places they'd been, churches he'd photographed. The Manchester ship canal gleamed like a silver knife cutting the countryside off his port wing. His vision started to blur again and he prayed 'Lord, keep my men safe. Please, let me land' he felt enormously sad. 'Bye Margot' he whispered, 'I love you.'

Silas held the stricken plane on course and offered a silent prayer of thanks as the undercarriage came down and locked.

On the airfield, people were emerging from bomb shelters. Cleveland nudged Pickmore 'what in hell's name is that?' he asked, pointing.

'Gawd' said Pickmore 'it's Jazzbohne's plane.'

Cleveland gawped at what looked like a flying scrap heap. 'How the hell's he flying that thang?'

The plane hit the grass heavily, bounced twice then settled. Silas's last conscious act was to shut down the engines. Sirens wailed as crash crews closed in.

Margot visited Silas every day. For a long while it was touch and go then, slowly, he began to recover. Two months later they wed in St Elphin's church where a proud Brian gave his daughter away. Silas's seed was growing within her.

Postscript:

2016. In the churchyard of St Elphin's Silas Terrence Jazzbohne the third, RAF fighter pilot, looked at the new tombstone with admiration. He was proud of the courageous life his grandparents had led. They'd run pubs in and around Warrington, countering every prejudice with great dignity, winning the hearts of all but the meanest. Before they'd passed on, two days apart in their nineties, they'd seen attitudes change dramatically. They'd played no small part in that change, helping make Warrington and the world a better place.

Justice for Jar Head

JoJo 'Jarhead' Jackson planned his raid on his neighbour with care. A prolific thief, he had never been caught since he was fourteen years old. Now, aged twenty-two he was an old hand at this kind of raid. Old people were his exclusive target, the older the better. They went to bed early and slept soundly. Most were deaf and had poor eyesight. They couldn't fight, they couldn't run and were terrified of burglars. That, in Jarhead's book, made them ideal targets.

Jarhead watched the old man through the knothole he'd pushed in the dividing fence, his forehead resting on the rough scratchy timber. The strong smell of creosote irritated his nostrils. He stifled a sneeze, well, most of it anyway a small t'choo escaped him. Had Benson heard it? Probably not, the old sucker was eighty-one for god's sake

Jarhead watched Benson sloshing on the foul-smelling liquid on for the whole of the last week. He'd offered to do it for him for fifty bucks, but Benson had politely refused. 'It keeps me out of mischief' the old man had joked, his leathery face wrinkling like an old boot. He winked, 'at my age yer gotta keep outta mischief. That blocked that avenue of discovering the old man's security arrangements so now he'd have to observe carefully and take notes. Just because his victims were elderly didn't mean he could afford to be lax. He had never been caught because he always made meticulous plans. Observation, planning and ruthless execution he told himself was the key to success Benson came home the same time every Wednesday evening after

his visit to the Veterans' club where he played five card stud poker with other vets. He had a reputation for always winning

Wednesday night, 11 p.m. The security light had come on sun-bright as Benson approached his door illuminating all the way down the long gravel drive to the street. He looked around carefully, yes he just might be seen from the road. He walked around the back to get a close-up inspection. The wooden windows were in good repair but the back door was flimsy.

Jarhead had seen enough and went back into his house. Up in his room, he assembled his tools. Ski mask, gloves, duct tape, air rifle, WD 40, screwdriver, short tyre lever and the hunting knife.

Next Wednesday morning, as dawn was breaking, Jarhead took the WD 40 and the loaded the air rifle, he then he shot a small squirt of the oil down filling the lead pellet. The friction of compressed air would cause the oil to explode when fired giving the pellet extra power. Enough to penetrate the security light's glass and knock out the bulb. He stood back from his bedroom window so the Phutt sound of the gun wouldn't carry far. His shot struck home boring a smooth hole. No spilt glass to give the game away. He smiled with cold satisfaction, the thrill of it always made his heart race.

Now he crept downstairs fearful of waking his parents who were sleeping off their night's excesses of alcohol in the next room.

In his stockinged feet he walked up to Benson's back door and squirted WD40 into the lock then, careful not to use too much, he oiled the hinges. If he was caught now he could claim he was just doing the old boy a favour.

Benson would be out when he raided but Jar Head was afraid the noisy old door could alert Peter, Benson's huge college football playing Grandson in the adjoining house. Jarhead would hate to mix it with him.

Jarhead watched the old man crunch his way slowly down the gravel and turn up the road to his club. Right, he thought, his diamond-sharp blue eyes narrowing. Half an hour until it's fully dark, then in I go. He touched the knife at his belt for reassurance, he climbed the fence into the zone of the security light. I failed to illuminate him as expected. He crept along the wall to the back of Benson's house. There he paused, listening for a full minute. All he heard was two cats screeching a few gardens away.

The door opened soundlessly. Great. He drew the knife as a precaution and entered the den. Crossing to a sideboard he was dazzled as the lights came on.

Benson was sitting in a winged armchair a relaxed look on his face.

'Hi Jarhead, do come in. Make yourself at home.'

The man stood and stared as total shock gripped him. 'How? How the hell is this possible?' He said, startled 'I,… I saw you go out…..'

Benson smiled grimly 'You sure did but then I looped around and came through the back door.'

'How did you know Benson?' he asked, removing his ski mask.

'Observation, Jarhead, observation.' He folded his hands in his lap. 'You see, back in the Korean war, I was a sniper. Snipers are trained to be ultra-observant and I've been observing you for a while now. I thought this day would come and it has.'

Jarhead's mouth was going up and down, but only spluttering sounds were emerging.

'Every time there has been a burglary in the district, Jarhead, you spent money the next day, New trainers or new Jeans, watch, a bike you name it, yet you don't work, neither do your folks. You offer to paint my fence, yet you've never done a day's work in your life. My fence suddenly had a knot fall out of it when it wasn't loose, I examined them all as I creosoted. Then you shot out the security light. Big mistake.

You see, with this kind of light a buzzer sounds in the house when it's activated. You should have shot out the Infra-red detector not the bulb. Oh, yeah, and thank you for oiling my lock I've been meaning to do it for ages. The old man eyed him, his grey eyes cold and hard, his posture relaxed. 'You should be more observant Jarhead.'

The burglar was regaining his composure now and advanced on Benson, face contorted, knife to the fore 'This ain't over yet you old fart, one thing I am is ruthless Benson, I don't mind killing old bastards like you.'

Benson's relaxed hand now drew a snub-nosed .38 from between his thighs. He aimed at Jarhead's chest. The man froze, dropped the knife and raised his hands. 'Don't shoot Benson, I surrender.'

'You know, Jarhead,' Benson said calmly 'the trouble with some ruthless bastards is that sometimes they run away with the idea that they are the only ruthless bastards.'

Jarhead looked nervous now, his dry mouth twitch spasmodically 'You,…you gonna call the cops, Benson?'

'No' said Benson 'put your mask back on.'

'What for man, you know who I am.'

'Put it on or I'll blow your balls off,' he lowered his aim. The click as he drew back the hammer sounded as loud as a church bell to Jarhead.

'Ok, Ok, man, anything you say, Ok.'

When the mask was replaced Benson fired, shooting Jarhead in the groin and blowing his manhood out the back of his Jeans.

Jarhead fell shrieking in agony and horror clutching himself, trying desperately to stem the flow of blood as he rolled around, eyes bulging.

Jarhead's screams gradually reduced to pain-racked sobs as tears of self-pity soaked his ski mask, 'ya gotta call an ambulance man. Ya gotta. Please.'

Benson ignored the pleas 'you see, Jarhead, he said in the same conversational tone as before 'snipers have to be ruthless, too. I was credited with 171 confirmed kills' said Benson calmly 'so I'm just gonna sit here quietly and enjoy watching you die. Your agonised death will, in some small way, make atonement for the untold misery you have selfishly inflicted on others.'

Jarhead pleaded some more but his life was ebbing as blood loss and shock took their toll.

When it was over Benson rang 911, affecting a quavering 'old man' voice, 'help, oh please help me officer, A burglar in a ski mask armed with a big knife just broke in and attacked me. I shot him, officer, and I think he's dead. Oh, dear, whatever am I to do?'

A Place to Rest

'Step it up there Jones582 my old granny moves livelier than you boy' roared Company Sergeant Major Evans.

Why don't you get off my back Evans you miserable bastard? Jones thought as he quickly caught up his place.

The sun had been beating on their backs like a leaden bar all day. They'd rested briefly and had eaten a frugal meal at noon before moving swiftly on. Jones 582 felt sweat running down his face in salty rivulets and tanging on his lips. Yet again wiped his brow on the coarse red wool of his sleeve. The sweat-stink from his soaking armpits offended him. His throat burned with the red dust kicked up by the Company's boots but his water had to last all day, so he bore it stoically.

In his Regiment, there were so many Jones's, that the soldier's last three digits of his army number had to be appended to his name in order to distinguish them. It felt dehumanising although he could never have expressed it that way.

Squinting at the sun Jones reckoned it was now getting on for four. He pushed his thumbs under the sodden shoulder straps of his heavy pack and eased the weight to a place that hurt a little less. 'God, how much longer? What godforsaken hole are we going this time? Why does no bugger ever tell us anything? He muttered under his breath. His ill-fitting boots rubbing his feet with every step, he'd have a couple more blisters by the end of today. He felt deep a depression sink through his soul as he trudged onward.

As the sun dipped horizonward Jones582 saw a small settlement coming into view. He felt a deep sense of relief as the officer walked his horse over to Evans. 'We're staying there Sah'nt Majah.' he drawled, nodding towards the cluster of buildings, his upper-class accent sounding alien to Jones's Welsh ear, few men had had any contact with the upper echelon of society before joining the army.

'Yessah' bawled the CSM "I'll send a scouting party forward, sah, and a runner to the baggage wagons to prepare your kit sah!"

The officer casually waved his swagger stick in return of his subordinate's smart salute and rode away.

Half an hour later Jones582's mood had changed dramatically as he prepared his bedroll. 'This must have been a cowshed judging by the smell and the dried shit on the floor, Daffid' he said to his friend Jones237, 'the roof's good and that bastard Evans hasn't detailed us for guard duty tonight.'

'A great billet to be sure Thomas, and a lovely place, to rest, too' said Jones237 with enthusiasm. A sound roof, good walls and a dry floor were great luxuries to be treasured by these men. No matter they were crammed in cheek by jowl is was much better than sleeping in the open.

The smell of boiling meat wafted to Jones582 from the company cauldron and after the long day's march, he was ravenous. He breathed a sigh of contentment. Great, a cushy billet, clean my rifle and kit then after my meal, a smoke, oh yes, at last, a smoke. He dug the clay pipe out of his pack happy to see it was intact. Then, at last, a good night's sleep, The newly swept floor was sandy and not too hard so he scraped a small pit for his hip. Oh God, how he relished the thought of sleep. Maybe in the morning they'd get a bathing party together and go to the nearby river, but that was too far ahead to think about now.

'Have you seen the land here' asked Jones237 'a man could stay in a place like this forever' he said in his musical Valley's lilt.

'Do you reckon so Daffid?'

'Oh, yes man, just look at that grass boyo' said Daffid his diamond blue eyes shining brightly 'A man could raise cattle, sheep, crops, anything he chose to here.'

'Hmnnn…it's very remote, I can't see a wife liking it Daffid.'

'A good Christian wife follows her husband without question as directed by the Bible' retorted Daffid sharply.

'Oh, please, Daffid' said Jones582 fervently, his mouth turning down at the corners, 'don't start bloody bible bashing now boyo, it's been a long day.'

Just when he thought nothing could save him from a Thomas237's bible lesson he was rescued by the Officer strolling by on his way to inspect his horse. Jones237 sprang to the door, stood up to attention and saluted 's'cuse me sah, permission to speak sah?'

The officer was mildly surprised but indulged the bright-eyed private. He recognised Jones237 as a solo tenor in the regimental choir and a good, deeply religious soldier 'yes, Jones, what is it?' he asked briskly.

'I was just wondering sah, this place is so beautiful a man could stay here forever, sah.'

The English officer was used to his Welsh soldiers waxing lyrical. 'A regiment of bloody poets and choristers' his father had said on learning his son had been seconded to them 'but there's some say they can fight a bit.' he had added grudgingly.

The officer looked around him noticing for the first time that the soldier was right. In the fiery blaze of the setting African sun, there was an air of great tranquillity. The undulating land looked fecund and productive as the long sweet grass waved in the cooling evening breeze. The lengthening shadows were rapidly imposing nightfall's claim casting deep purple shadows. It irritated him that a common soldier would notice such great beauty before he himself who was born of the land-owning gentry.

'If you have a question for God's sake spit it out, man.'

'I'm writing home tonight sir, I was wondering what's today's date and does this beautiful place have a name, sir?'

The officer glowered at Jones237 standing stiffly to attention 'It's the twenty-first of January Jones and this place of absolutely no consequence and even less charm is known locally as Kwajimu. We call it Rorke's Drift.'

Historical note:

At the Battle of Rorke's Drift on 22nd Jan 1879 139 soldiers of "B" Company the 2nd Battalion 24th of Foot drove off 4,000+ Zulu warriors winning 11 Victoria Crosses, Britain's highest award for bravery, in the process. (6 before breakfast) That record still stands as the highest number ever awarded for a single battle.

It is sometimes said that modern rifles were easily used against 'poor natives with short spears' however, it has been claimed that none of the soldiers killed that day died of stab wounds; all were shot by the Zulus many of whom were armed with old but serviceable rifles.

The battle inspired the film Zulu starring Michael Cain. The regiment was not, as the film portrayed, an exclusively Welsh regiment at that time.

A STING IN THE TALE

Blind Date

Melanie poured herself a stiff drink then slumped disconsolately into her armchair. 'Bugger' she said aloud. Taking a large swig, she began raking over her first and last date with Jackson Jones. He'd been pleasant enough, a good-humoured soul who'd made her laugh. But she knew as soon as she'd heard his first 'oh, hello' that he was shocked. He covered it better than most of her dates, but it was unmistakably there. Confirmation had come at the end of the date when he said 'well, good night Melanie, I'll ring you next week.'

She heard her front door open 'Cooee Melanie it's only me love, how did it go?'

'Same as it always does Aunty June' she said sounding dejected 'pleasant enough but "I'll give you a ring" was all I got at the end.'

Aunt June scratched her unworldly greying head in exasperation. A decent woman in her early fifties she was desperate to help her twenty-four-year-old niece find a suitable young man. Oh dear, she thought, a deep sense of disappointment taking hold of her. 'I don't understand it' she mused 'you're as

167

pretty as a picture, your figure is great and as for your legs; wow!'

'Aunty June, I'm blind. No one wants to go out with me they see me as some sort of liability' she sniffled and blew her nose 'I suppose I'll just have to get used to the idea I'll always be on my own.'

June felt an ache sweep over her heart like a wave crashing onto rocks. her sweet face crumpled like a wet paper sack. She had arranged this date through an agency. 'Didn't you tell him when you spoke on the phone last night dear?'

'Of course, I didn't' said Melanie irritated, 'didn't you tell the agency?'

June felt a deep pang in her heart and her voice wavered 'no dear, I didn't, I thought...Oh, dear, I thought I'd leave that to you when he rang you.' her voice trailed away to silence.

'If I tell a bloke I'm blind before I meet him he usually puts me off straight away or, worse still, stands me up. Her bright blue unseeing eyes brimmed with tears, she felt on the verge of despair 'no matter how pretty I may or may not be Aunty June, nobody wants to date a blind girl. Please, just leave it, OK?"

A month passed before Aunt June raised the subject of boys again this time about a really special boy. Melanie cut her off abruptly 'I don't want to know Aunty June, it'll end like all the others. Leave it, please, just leave it.'

'Yes, Melanie, but......'

'No, no, no,' Melanie shouted 'No, June, and that's final. Just drop it will you?'

June felt a piercing hurt in her breast and her whole body shook but held her peace when she saw just how upset Melanie was. Over coffee, they chatted about mutual friends, the weather and other things but avoided mentioning men. Just before she left, June said 'It's not like you to give up Melanie. When your mum died and you moved in here on your own everyone expected you to fail. You didn't.'

Melanie sighed, June was right about that. How's she going to cope without her mum? was the question well-meaning friends had asked each other. Without her mother caring for her, she'll be unable to cope seemed to be the general consensus. Well, they were all wrong she thought defiantly. Totally, utterly bloody wrong.

On leaving June turned in the doorway weighed down with guilt 'look, I'm sorry Melanie but I gave him, Peter that is, your number....... he may not ring though....he's very shy.....the thing is....'

'Oh, good god June' Melanie almost exploded with frustration. She omitted the Aunty title to show her annoyance 'and I suppose you told him I was a poor hapless little blind girl who was desperate for company? I'll bloody well send him packing if he rings, so there!'

'No. Oh dear, no Melanie I didn't tell...' June

169

choked, unable to continue. Bursting into tears she turned and fled her niece's hostility.

Melanie felt bad about having shouted at her dear Aunty June who was, after all, only trying her best to help her. She would ring her later and apologise. If she rang now she knew they'd both end in floods of tears. She felt lower than at any time she could remember.

Peter rang that evening and to her surprise, she was immediately taken by his gentle melodic Hebridean Scots accent. His voice had a soft musical lilt that made her want to listen forever. He told her he was twenty-seven, from Stornoway on the Isle of Lewis that he sang in a choir and loved animals. His crystal-clear voice sounded like an angel singing in her ear. She felt her heart beating faster but, with an effort, held herself in check. Too many times her hopes had been dashed. Intrigued as she was, though, she kept the call brief, giving away scant few personal details. They agreed to meet outside McDonald's the next day. 'And only for coffee, OK?' she had said emphatically.

Melanie woke early next day feeling excited in spite of herself. She showered then dressed with extra care wanting to look her best for him this man with the golden voice. Just before she left she knelt and said a little prayer 'Please, Lord, help me' she pleaded a desperate longing flooding her every fibre 'since mum died you know how lonely I've been.

Just for once, Lord, just this once let me find some happiness.'

She got off the number thirty-two bus in the town square and made her way to the crossing. She waited for the beeping signal then crossed. In her head, she counted the steps walking briskly, confidently, sweeping her white cane rapidly before her. It was her way of telling the world I don't need your help, or your pity thank you. Seventy-two paces to the precinct turn right mind the rubbish bin at fifty-eight paces. Carry on for another one hundred and four and bingo she was there.

The balled tip of her cane lightly touched a shoe her heightened hearing detecting a slight nervous intake of breath. 'Are you Peter?' she asked.

'Yes, and you'll be Melanie?

Yes, shall we go in, Peter?

'Sure, c'mon Jess.'

'Who's Jess?' asked Melanie suspiciously.

'Why? Can't you see? She's my guide dog.'

The Stalker

'Oi, you.' he called, coming up behind her with huge, balaclava-clad head and waving arm. The rain-laden wind whipped his overcoat about his legs and the solitary street light threw his shadow long on the cold wet pavement.

Nine pm, the business district was deserted she cast about for a taxi, a car to flag down, anything, anyone, desperate to escape the approaching spectre.

Janet had been working overtime, yet again, trying to pay off her rent arrears, walking home to save taxi fare. Now she feared it would be her undoing, a terrible mistake.

Her knees turned to jelly, and she backed away, clutching her arms around her trembling body only to find herself cringing in the corner of an unlit bus shelter. She was utterly trapped.

On he came, slowly, inexorably, a menacing giant. He entered her personal space before he stopped, looming over her. His foul body odour seemed to permeate every fibre of her being. She felt nauseated. Stale tobacco stench oozed from his broken yellow/brown teeth and invaded her lungs. She felt vomit churning.

'I watch's you every night from that doorway, pretty lady' he said in a dull monotone, 'then I follows yer' his voice was a slow, his huge, dark staring eyes were mesmerizing.

Oh, please, God, she silently prayed, not this, *please,* not this. 'Oh, sir, please, I've, … I've got some money.,.. you, you can have it' She fumbled through her pockets with urgent, trembling hands.

'I Don't want yer money, pretty lady' he said as his hand slowly reached out towards her breast. Janet began to wet herself. 'please…*oh please*….' she whimpered, don't…'.

'Anyway, you got no money, 'cos you dropped this.'

She tore her eyes from his hypnotic stare to see he was holding out her purse.

He thrust it into her trembling hand, 'I follows yer to see that you gets to the busy streets safe, pretty lady, I used to be a soldier yer knows.'

Without waiting for thanks, the old homeless man turned and shuffled back to his doorway.

'G'night pretty lady' he called.

The Gods of the Odds

As a serial killer, Royston Bains was very successful. A quiet little man barely five feet tall, Bains was, he believed, a genius. He went through life largely ignored by his fellow man. At forty-five, he was still single, living with his invalid mother. Men ignored him, women didn't even see him. His desire to kill, to gain revenge on a world that failed to recognise his genius was all consuming.

Bains carefully studied the routine of one Kayden Norris. He knew he hung around the Chorlton Street bus station until around ten p.m. then cruised Canal Street's gay village, taking clients for a short walk down the dark canal towpath.

Bains accosted Norris on the towpath away from security cameras. He gave him twenty pounds telling him to walk down the towpath and meet him at his car in a nearby side street. 'Meet me there and there'll be another thirty for you.'

Kayden smiled knowingly 'married are you, pal? Scared you'll be seen with me?'

'Do you want the business or not?'

'Yeah, yeah, mate, OK. I'll see you there in five minutes.'

Bains knew the CCTV camera covering the side street wasn't working because he'd hacked the system and switched it off. His car was a ten-year-old Peugeot estate now sporting the number plates of a similar vehicle. The route to the murder spot had been carefully chosen.

In his fifteen-year career of slaughter, Bains had never even been a suspect. This underlined what he already knew, that he was a true genius. He worked out the chances of being caught before each kill. He kept the gods of the odds firmly on his side. The police needed evidence. He gave them none.

Unsuspecting, Norris followed Bains into the bushes on the wasteland to perform the sex act that he'd been paid for. The boy knelt as Bains fiddled with his fly.

The lad looked up, his handsome face creased 'God, mate, first you don't want to do it in your nice warm car, now you can't even open your fly Here, let me do it' he said pulling down the zip with ease. 'No need to be nervous mate, I'm an expert' he looked down, leaning forward to deliver his service.

Bains slid the cutthroat razor from his pocket and, placing one hand firmly on the boy's head, he slipped the razor under his chin and slashed his throat with one lightning, stroke.

The boy fell back, his bulging eyes staring up at his killer, both hands clutching at the wound, his mouth screamed soundlessly as his lifeblood gushed from between his fingers. His last blurred vision was of his killer's calm, smiling face.

'For what it's worth, filth, you're my eighteenth.' He bent and retrieved his money. As he stood for a moment looking down at his latest victim, Bains felt cheated. It had been just too easy, he'd not derived his usual satisfaction. Perhaps he needed a bigger challenge?

Bains saw the news reports on the death of Kayden Norris. Police put the savage murder down to a revenge killing because Kayden had owed money to several drug dealers. His red-eyed mother made the usual T.V. appeal extolling her late son's saintly virtues then the whole affair sank into the obscurity of unsolved crime.

*****

'I'm off to the computer club mummy' he called from the front door.

'Must you go and leave me all alone Royston? His disabled mother whined.

'It's Friday mummy, you know it's Friday.' She didn't answer, just sulked, he never missed his Friday nights out.

Bains always put an extra sleeping pill in her cocoa before he went out, she'd be fast asleep in five minutes, as she also was whenever he went a killing mission.

Talking computing, hacking techniques and other

techy stuff to his two geeky friends Pete and Dave made his week. Working in I.T security for a large insurance company paid well but bored him. His everyday interest was in hacking, his hobby was murder.

Bains had, with his usual care, laid the foundations of his next murder six months previously. He had joined a dating website and had met with several women. All his dates had ended in disappointment due to his introverted personality and, he thought, his lack of height. Girls, he believed, despised short men. One girl, though, Sally Oldfield, was different. She was pretty, vain and had an appetite for expensive foreign holidays, meals in top restaurants and not-so-subtle flattery. Her online profile had many photos displaying her fine figure. Her face, though beautiful, looked haughty.

His online profile was that of a successful thirty-something businessman who ran a successful IT company. He described himself as 'solvent' and a lover of the finer things in life. In his one profile picture, taken years earlier, he was wearing a business suit. against a neutral background. His carefully constructed persona exuded prosperity without any vulgar boasting.

They met at an up-market restaurant in Alderley Edge, a haunt of minor celebrities and football stars. With champagne, the bill came to a small fortune, but Royston Bains didn't flinch. He readily proffered his credit card and left a generous cash tip, too.

Sally was impressed. OK, so he was quiet, a short arse and looked out of place walking beside her. She stood five-foot-ten in her heels. No matter, he obviously had money and was prepared to spend it. He could be the means by which she could open her dreamed of beauty salon.

Bains drove her home afterwards in a brand-new five series BMW he had hired for the occasion. He did not push her to let him come in for coffee. Another date followed to much the same pattern this time ending with passionate kissing and a grope, Sally allowed nothing more. She knew how to play men.

Bains didn't make another date telling Sally he was away on a business trip for a month and would contact her on his return. He didn't, and he left the dating site.

Sally put it down to experience and moved on with her life.

*****

'Hi, Sally, remember me? Royston?

'Yeah, hey, where have you *been*? Why did you leave the site?'

He was silent for a couple of seconds when he spoke again his voice was sombre. 'My mother died' he lied 'I've been feeling a bit down since then. We were very close you know.'

'Oh, God, I'm so sorry Royston.'

He let her ramble on about condolences for a few moments listening carefully for any hint of disbelief in her voice. There was none.

'Listen, Sally, the reason I rang you tonight is to see if you'd be up for a holiday in Dubai next month?' He heard her catch her breath. 'I was thinking about a suite at that Burj Al Arab hotel, you know the one?

'Wow, yes, I'll say' she responded eagerly 'but doesn't that place charge an absolute fortune?'

His voice was serious 'that won't be a problem Sally you see I have had a bit of luck. You are the first and only person I've told, and I want it kept strictly secret, you understand?'

'Er, I think so Royston, tell me more' her excitement was growing now, and she felt a tingle run down her spine.

'OK, Sally, but you mustn't tell a single soul, the last thing I need is publicity and begging letters, people knocking on my door, that sort of thing.' He paused allowing her to put two and two together.

Her voice sounded uncertain but with an unmistakable note of excitement 'are we talking about a lottery win or something, Royston?'

'Are you alone?'

'Yes.'

'It's not a huge win by lottery standards, just two point six million, but I don't want it bandied about, not even to your closest friends, OK?'

'I won't say a word, Royston' she gushed 'I promise, honestly.'

The addition of the word 'honestly' told him that as soon as he was off the phone she'd confide, in strictest confidence, of course, in her favourite girlfriend, thus ensuring the world and his wife would know by next day. He had to prevent her talking about him at all costs. His voice became brittle 'listen, Sally' he snapped, I'm deadly serious here. If I see one word on social media, hear one piece of stray gossip then the whole damned thing is off, you understand? There'll be no going back, and you'll never hear from me again.'

She took a sharp breath; her knuckles whitening around her phone. Maybe he wasn't such a malleable mug after all. 'OK, Royston, but I'll have to tell them sometime, won't I?'

'You can tell them about the holiday, but only after it's all booked and finalised, right? The win stays secret.'

'OK, I promise, and I mean it, too.' she sounded genuinely sincere 'what's the next step Royston?'

'I'll bring some brochures over tomorrow night, Sally. I have a business meeting in Crewe, a long-term commitment. The guy's a friend as well as a client. I can't just let him down. I'll phone you around seven. I'll book that nice restaurant again, OK?'

Sally readily agreed and went to bed that night feeling thrilled. She longed to tell her mother, but she knew her mother would tell her sister. Auntie Belle was an avid user of social media and a bigger gossip than even her mum. No, she'd wait until tomorrow and, with luck, secure her future.

When Sally received a call from a strange number next day she hesitated before answering.

'Hi Sally, it's me, Royston. Look, something's come up. I'll be delayed an hour, sorry. I rang you on my business phone because I forgot my personal one, dammit. God, I've had a helluva day' he moaned, 'nothing's gone to plan. The BMW broke down, some bloody electrical gizmo they have to order, and the only car they could loan me is an old Peugeot, I'm up to my ears, but I'll see you soon and we'll relax and forget all this sodding nonsense, OK?'

'What about the restaurant, Royston?'

'No problem. I rang them. They were very good about it, but I want to show you these brochures first and decide which suite we're having. It wouldn't be right to do that in the restaurant. It would look a bit flash, like we were trying to impress or something.' He gave her the location of a walkers' carpark near the Edge.

'It's a bit remote, isn't it?

'Remote? Don't be silly, it's on my way' he said impatiently 'last time I was there it was packed with bloody dog walkers.' He paused 'oh, sod it, I'm wrapping up this damned business now, I'll be there in twenty minutes, OK?' He hung up without waiting for an answer, pleased with his performance. He'd played the harassed businessman to a tee.

Sally arrived on time and he watched as her red Mini circled the empty carpark until her headlights found his Peugeot. He waved the glossy brochure through the window, beaming a huge smile. She waved back, hurrying to climb in. The ligature was hidden behind the literature.

After stuffing her body into the boot of her Mini and locking it, Bains started on his pre-planned route down remote, camera-free country lanes All had gone perfectly, she had suspected nothing, bending over the brochure on his lap as drew the sash cord around her slender neck and jerked it tight. Her look of horrified shock delighted him, her fierce struggle, legs kicking, fingers clutching desperately, uselessly at the rope as he slowly choked the life from her. It gave him an erection.

Preoccupied with reliving the murder, he made a wrong turn in the hard-to-follow back lanes. He was heading south not north. He cursed himself inwardly. He'd never bought a Satnav; a genius doesn't make mistakes.

He reached the motorway at Holmes Chapel putting miles on his journey and turned north.

He'd been on the motorway for about five

minutes when the Peugeot started spluttering. The engine died then picked up again, but his speed was reduced.

Knutsford service station was coming up and he sighed with relief as the car staggered into the first available space just inside the huge parking area before conking out altogether. Only one other car was near. Far away was the brightly lit centre.

He sat there cursing that he wasn't a member of a recovery service. He'd thrown away the cheap phone he'd bought for the murder after removing the sim card and burying it in a layby. His own phone was at home, part of any potential alibi he may need. He was stuck. If he went into the service station to use a public phone, then he'd be on camera.

He looked gloomily under the bonnet, his brain working frantically, a sick feeling in the pit of his stomach replacing his earlier euphoria. He had to get home before his mother awoke otherwise she'd know he'd been out.

'Are you having trouble'?

Bains turned. In the dim light, he couldn't decide if the person was a boyish-looking girl or a girlish looking boy.

'Oh, yes, this damned wreck has broken down and I'm not a member of a recovery service.'

'Where are you going?'

'Manchester.'

'Me, too, I'll give you a lift if you like.'

'Are you sure? I mean, you're on your own and you don't know me from Adam.'

The person smiled reassuringly, even at close range he still couldn't determine the sex. The voice was light and neutral.

This was a godsend. He could slide into a car no one would associate him with and get out of his predicament. He could report his car stolen in the morning. 'That's very generous of you' he said, 'very kind indeed.'

As he slid into the passenger seat he decided his benefactor was a woman. 'May I ask your name?'

'I'm Kim, Kim Jones 'she said and in case you're wondering, which I know you are, I was born into a woman's body, but now I'm in transition. Does that bother you?' The arched eyebrow told him it had better not.

'No, not at all, Kim. I'm Richard Mason by the way. She shook his hand her grip firm. They drove off.

'What do you do Richard?' she queried, her voice friendly.

'I'm a writer' he lied for an in-house computer company magazine, awfully boring I'm afraid.'

She smiled, 'I 'm a rep for a wholesale sex toy company would you believe?' She laughed and went on to chat about her job telling him amusing anecdotes of cheeky executives asking for a demonstration.

It was as she chatted he thought what about two killings in a single night? She's such an easy target and no one knew he was with her. He tried to dismiss the idea, he'd done no research or planning. But she was a potential witness, she could place him at Knutsford. This gnawed at his brain like a rabid rat. It could be done his inner voice said, the gods of the odds are with you, just get her to pull over on the pretext of wanting a pee. A quick chop to the throat would disable her then he could use her underwear to finish the job. The thought excited him, and his loins stirred. Wow! He'd wanted a challenge, now he had one.

'Do you often give lifts to strangers? He asked as they passed through the southernmost outskirts of the city, I mean, I could be a serial killer for all you know.'

She laughed heartily at this, glancing sideways at him. He could see by the dashboard light that she was amused.

'Oh, I don't think so Richard' she said merrily, 'you look the harmless type that's why I gave you a lift. You looked so small, lost and vulnerable standing by your car, I simply had to help you.'

Bains didn't answer, his anger rising. Harmless? Small? Vulnerable? What a patronising bitch! Yes, he would kill this woman, this stupid woman-cum-man who was too dumb to know when she was in danger.

ANTHONY MILLIGAN

They were deeper in the outskirts now, an area he knew well. 'I'm sorry Kim but I need to pee quite badly, there's a small industrial estate just along here, it'll be quiet now. Do you mind if we pull in?' He drew his knees up like a man desperate for the lavatory. He thought she looked hesitant. He screwed his face up 'I'm afraid I have a medical condition and when I need to go, I have to.'

She nodded her understanding and turned into the rundown estate, stopping by a rubbish-filled skip. It was dark and gloomy a single lamp at the entrance cast long shadows.

Inside, Bains was seething. He turned to her. 'I really am a serial killer you know, I was on my way back from killing a woman in Alderley Edge when I broke down. She was my nineteenth victim.' His manner was deadly serious, but Kim just laughed in his face.

'Why don't you bloody well believe me? You stupid bitch' he screamed.

Kim smiled benignly, 'you good at maths, Richard? What are the odds against two serial killers meeting accidentally and sharing a car?'

He heard the sharp click as her knife flicked open, saw the flash of steel as death pierce his chest.

She leaned across, kissed his cheek, then opened his door 'bloody little fantasist' she laughed. She twisted the knife and withdrew as she pushed him out 'you're my twenty-first by the way.'

Kim drove off laughing crazily, two untraceable murders in one night. Wow, she thought, what were the odds of achieving that?

She'd burn the stolen car in Wythenshawe Park with its dead owner the boot. Then take the bus home. Her favourite sex toy would take a severe pounding later. Kim's underwear was wet in anticipation.

She was laughing in a state of high euphoria. Her foot pressed the accelerator. She failed to see the red light or the tram that killed her.

The Gods of the odds, it seems, are fickle.

If you've enjoyed at least some of these stories, please let me know on

ppap.writeme@gmail.com

If you didn't enjoy them let me know that, too.

If you would be kind enough review my work on Amazon, I would be very grateful. Just say what you honestly think, that is all I ask.

Thanks for reading.

36093837R00110

Printed in Poland
by Amazon Fulfillment
Poland Sp. z o.o., Wrocław